Alfred Austin

Fortunatus the Pessimist

Second Edition

Alfred Austin

Fortunatus the Pessimist
Second Edition

ISBN/EAN: 9783337266899

Printed in Europe, USA, Canada, Australia, Japan

Cover: Foto ©Andreas Hilbeck / pixelio.de

More available books at **www.hansebooks.com**

FORTUNATUS THE PESSIMIST

BY

ALFRED AUSTIN

SECOND EDITION

London

MACMILLAN AND CO.

AND NEW YORK

1892

First Edition printed November 1892

Second Edition December 1892

PERSONAGES

FORTUNATUS . . . . *An English Duke.*

ADRIAN . . *His Friend and Secretary.*

FRANKLIN . . . . *A Yeoman.*

URANIA . . . *His Daughter.*

APRIL . . . . . *A Forest Foundling.*

ABADDON . . . . . *A Pedlar.*

PLACE.

The Duke's Castle—Urania's Garden—The Forest.

TIME—To-day.

ACT I

SCENE I

[The terrace of the DUKE'S castle.   FORTUNATUS, with ADRIAN
at his side, and a number of domestics behind.   A crowd
of Rustics approach.]

RUSTIC.

Sir, shall we sing?

FORTUNATUS.

Ay, let us hear you.

ADRIAN (*raising his hand*).

Now!

The PLOUGHMEN *sing.*

Three cheers for Winter,
That blows upon the horn,

B

That makes the branches splinter,
   And threshes out the corn :
When chimney-stacks are shaken,
   And flooded is the ditch,
And the gammer salts the bacon,
   And the lasses sit and stitch,
Or thread the melted tallow
   To cheer the longsome nights,
And the ploughland oozeth fallow,
   And the black frost nips and bites ;
When we close and bar the shutter,
   As the wet winds wail and sob,
And we watch the chestnuts sputter
   And crackle on the hob ;
When the Yule log lights the rafter,
   And the gossip tells the tale,
And the house is filled with laughter,
   And the mugs are filled with ale :
         Three cheers for Winter !

The SHEPHERDS *sing.*

Three cheers for Springtime,
   That makes the pastures strong,

When, blithe upon the wing, Time
    Comes bursting into song :
When celandine and oxslip
    Are dotted all about,
And the young ones on their frocks slip,
    And sally forth and shout ;
When lifted is the wattle,
    And emptied is the shed,
And the dewy-fetlocked cattle
    Roam afield for board and bed ;
When we ply the rake and harrow,
    And bark the oaken bole,
And the lean sow drops her farrow,
    And the broodmare drops her foal ;
When the buxom lambs are bleating,
    And the cuckoo never stops,
And the glad swain and his sweeting
    Are cuddling in the copse :
        Three cheers for Springtime !

The MOWERS *sing.*

Three cheers for Summer,
    When posies smell once more,

And morrice-man and mummer
   Come dancing to the door :
When open stands the casement,
   And walls that dripped with snow
Are hung from eave to basement
   With roses all ablow ;
When grass is scythed and tedded,
   And work is paid-for play,
And lad and lass are wedded,
   And tumble in the hay ;
When everything increases,
   And mother makes the jams,
While we shear the curly fleeces,
   And wean the lusty lambs ;
When the youngsters pitch the wicket
   Upon the village green,
And the elders watch the cricket,
   And talk of what hath been :
         Three cheers for Summer !

      The REAPERS *sing.*

Three cheers for Autumn,
   When jolly shocks of grain,

And the brawny arms that wrought 'em,
   Ride homeward on the wain ;
When the early rime-frost dapples
   The tender woodland leaves,
And the juicy ruddled apples
   Are stored behind the eaves ;
When unto green hop-garden
   Pour all the village folk,
And the cobnuts swell and harden,
   And the oasts are lit and smoke ;
When steams the harvest-supper
   With joints of beef and boar,
And lower dance with upper
   Upon the granary floor ;
When the yeoman counts his earning,
   And the yokel's wage is known,
And the maiden feels a yearning
   For a fireside of her own :
        Three cheers for Autumn !

      They ALL *sing.*

Then three cheers, my hearties,
   And together three times three,

For whatsoe'er your part is,
  Or whoso ye may be,
Be yours to spud the thistles,
  To scoop and bank the ditch,
To souse and scrape the bristles,
  And to cut up chine and flitch,
To peel and twist the withy,
  To tend the lambing ewe,
To smite upon the stithy
  And hammer out the shoe ;
To find the emmet maggots,
  To stake and tie the hops,
Or to stack the hazel faggots
  In spinney and in copse ;
To mount the market waggon,
  Or to whistle by the shaft,
Now lift the home-brewed flagon,
  And drain a goodly draught :
       With three cheers, my hearties !

FORTUNATUS.

A May-day tune, pitched in no whining key,
Nor sung to sorrow.   Feeling thus, you do
Wisely to rhyme not over-ruefully.

But, be the burden jocund or morose,
Singing is drouthy work.   Thanks then, and hence
To fill your windpipes with more melody,
Cool-casked within the cellar.

[The Rustics depart.]

                 There they go,
Jostling and joking; bellied with the ale
Brewed on my Birthday, when the Age was young.
Birthday or death-day, 'tis all one to them,
So it be marked with malt.   Bulged out with beer,
No devil's date they would not celebrate
As vocally as mine.

[The domestics retire.]

             Ah! hopeful Adrian,
There's more felicity in a tun of ale
Than all the Hedonists.   Twelve sweltering hours,
A sleep upon the settle then and there,
A wench to cuddle, and then ale, more ale;
These are the pleasures primitive that make
Invention folly, progress slavery,
Imposed by some taskmaster out of sight,
And our fastidious fineries the mirage
Of mortal travel.   Shall we go within?

SCENE II

[The DUKE's library.]

ADRIAN (*sitting at a table with papers before him*).

To-morrow, then, you leave this fair domain,
And journey townward?

FORTUNATUS.

Even so it is,
Since so it'must be.   Custom, like the moon,
This way and that swayeth the bitter course
Of sterile being.   You will come with me?

ADRIAN.

Gladly.   But there are matters, ere you go,
Exacting your attention.   These are they.
Will you dispatch them now?

FORTUNATUS.

Now will be then,
Would you but wait.   But, since I try your patience,

Scan we these unadministered bequests
From deceased yesterdays.   Why cannot Time,
Ebbing, rake back the litter of its flow,
Not leave it stranded?

ADRIAN.

                Time's foreshore is ours;
And we, the lords of opportunity,
May find a treasure from its unplumbed deep
Among the refuse.

FORTUNATUS.

                Thus you humour me,
Mending my mouldy metaphor.   So to work.
Of work or weariness we have our choice,
Mocking alternatives.   We prove the one,
To find the other better; bootless both,
Save to accelerate or retard the time
When neither load nor leisure wearies more.

ADRIAN.

Now shall we hear the vicar?

FORTUNATUS.

Yes, the Church;
Precedence for the Church.   The weakest first,
Weakest and most importunate.

ADRIAN.

He craves
For a new lectern.   .

FORTUNATUS.

What!   Is the old worn out?
Time makes an end sometimes of uselessness.

ADRIAN.

No: stolen from its place.   Some virtuoso,
Some lover of archaic furniture,
Fancied and filched it.

FORTUNATUS.

Give him then a new one,
The fellow of the old, and none will steal it.
Our unoriginal age collects the tools,
Spoons, corals, papboats, bellows, thuribles,
Of man's inventive childhood.   Simple vicar!

He is the veriest curio of them all,
He, not the lectern; and he lives and thrives
On this strange mania for the obsolete.
Give lectern, rood-screen, pulpit, altar-rails,
All, anything, he wills.

ADRIAN.

The belfry gapes.
At the last funeral-dirge the tiles slid down,
Albeit they tolled so gingerly.

FORTUNATUS.

They would
Have tumbled from the timbers, one and all,
Had they rung timely music.   Christening-bells,
And marriage-peals, shaken so wrongfully,
Should be reserved for requiems.   Then it is
We should rejoice, if ever.   Must man weep,
It should be at the cradle, not the grave.
Rebuild the belfry.

ADRIAN.

Next, the schoolmaster
Petitions for another wing.   The standards
Are crammed to overflowing.

FORTUNATUS.

　　　　　　Happy birds,
Unhappy urchins, in an age like ours !
Birdnesting's out of fashion.　Pothooks cramp
The hand that should be limber for the plough
And supple for the sickle.　I forgot.
Lecterns survive, sickles are out of date.
Give him two wings—he's sure to need them both,
The yokels breed so fast—to teach their brood
How fine it is to be a city clerk,
Scribe, politician, rogue, philanthropist,
While carting muckheaps is a scullion's work,
Hedging and ditching feudal servitude,
And porridge food for porkers.

ADRIAN.

　　　　　　You are asked
Will you adjudicate between the hands
That work the mines and those that lease them from
　　　you,
Anent the hours of work.　Those plead that eight
Suffice a day's existence underground.

FORTUNATUS.

Where do they plan to spend the rest, and how?
In yawning at the cross-ways, swopping pups,
Listening to shrill upbraiding from their wives,
Dazed on a bench or drunk upon the floor,
As little better for the sun as if
It never rose again, and all their days
Lapsed underground?   But, give them what they ask,
Till they ask more; then, give them that as well.

ADRIAN.

But the leaseholders of your mines aver
It will be equal to the royalty
They pay to you.

FORTUNATUS.

             The royalty foregone
Will make it even.   Answer yes to all,
And leave all thereby discontented still,
With satisfaction surfeited.   Our hinds,
Wiser than our mechanics, willing work
From dawn to dark, the changeful seasons through.
Unconsciously they copy Nature's pace,

And tick with Nature's minutes, solemn, slow,
Staid as their parlour-clocks.   She never stops,
Knowing that rest is wearier than fatigue ;
And they, who have no knowledge, imitate
The instinct they are suckled on.   Wise hinds,
Wise in the trudging ignorance that asks
No question or from life or death, but walks
Still at a funeral pace along the road
That ends, without a guide-post, at the grave.

ADRIAN.

Nay, hear *them* now.   The home-farm woodlanders
Ask sixpence more a cant, and billhooks shouldered
At five on Saturdays.

FORTUNATUS.

    Alas ! poor rustics !
They too have ta'en the virus of the time,
And sicken for more leisure to discover
The heaviest load of all is life itself,
Forgotten, or half felt not, by the backs
That bow beneath a faggot.   Conscious man
Is a poor fretful invalid that turns,
First on this side, then that, in hope to find

The other easier.   Luckless woodlanders !
They too demand more time for consciousness,
More leisure to be wretched.   Give it them ;
'Twere bootless to refuse.   More sick we are,
The more must we be humoured.

ADRIAN.

                              You remember

That in the shire there is a vacancy,
And each side craves your aid and influence.

FORTUNATUS.

Then give it to them both, and so increase
Their bootless passions still more bootlessly.
Of all our feigned affections, there is none
So hollow, selfish, and injurious,
As what we christen Patriotism.

ADRIAN (*lifting flowers out of a basket*).

                              Here are roses,

With morning dew upon their maiden faces,
Fair as the daughters they would fain have sent,
Who proffer these instead.

FORTUNATUS.

Ay, fairer still,

And scarce more fleeting.   Adrian, flowers are best.

While they are sweet, they are sweet, nothing but
    sweet,

And, when they fade, forgetfulness absorbs

Their beauty and our worship.   Woman wanes

Slowly, and still needs incense though the bloom

Hath vanished from the altar.

ADRIAN.

Here are gifts,

More numerous than your years, unscanned, unopened,

Though well I ween the givers are, themselves,

More often wooed than wooers.

FORTUNATUS.

The which spoils all.

There is no quality, how rich soe'er,

Bestowed by Fate, but straightway Fate itself

Will contradict its exercise and make

It void or venomous.   The hand that gives

Injures the hand that takes.   The rich, the great,

The mighty, the magnificent, are wooed,
Not for themselves; hence are not wooed at all.
Beauty from faithfulness absents its gaze,
To keep its eye on splendour.   'Tis a world
Where all is bought, and nothing's worth the price.
Now, may I go?

ADRIAN (*rising*).

                Yes! and the air of heaven
Waft to you saner thoughts!
                                    [*Exit* FORTUNATUS.

ADRIAN (*alone*).

                        Poor Fortunatus!
Poor in his boundless opulence and power.
Where got he this disease?   Better not ponder
Too deeply on that question, lest I too
Should fall a-moaning.   Against sickly thought,
Action's the prophylactic.

C

SCENE III

FORTUNATUS (*on horseback*).

On then, still on !   Swift motion for awhile
Dispels despondency ; but, when we pause,
How quickly, like a phial that contains
Some nauseous medicine, thought secretes anew
The sediment of sorrow.   Thus, when Man
Matures to meditation, and his blood
Slackens to foot-pace, plainly he discerns
The mockery of being.   Look on these woods !
Unto the eye of April, April flowers
Are fair because both lack significance ;
And April music unto April ears
Is sweet since meaningless.   Thought, final phase
Of that incorporated force which drives
Our carnal substance blindly onward, blurs
Nature's expressionless smooth passive face,
By making it our mirror, where we see
Reflected our desires, our dreams, our doubts,
With death for background ; death, lewd grinning
        satyr,
Who gloats on, with anticipating eyes,

The naked self-complacency of life.
The unmeditative primrose asks not why
It blooms then fades, nor doth the bluebell feel
The pathos of its passing ; but man comes,
And with unquiet questioning infects
The woodland with his woe.   The impulsive note
Sung by yon cuckoo conscienceless, when heard
By human ear, sounds like melodious guilt,
The mocking Mephistopheles of Love.
The nightingale that bubbleth 'mong the leaves
With such sweet insolicitude it asks
No dullard night to sleep away its song,
Misread by melancholy man, bewails
A woe it understands not, thoughtless bird.
Thus staid reflection's shadow falls athwart
The cheerful seeming of the Spring, and makes
May sadder than December.
                    [His horse stumbles.]
                              Nearly down !
Art tired, good beast ?   No, he hath cast a shoe.
So far, too, from his stall.
                    [A voice is heard singing.]

O, my lands are broad, and fat, and fair,
And fair and fat my beeves :

From dawn I ride till the day hath died

    Under my own green leaves.

But the leaf turns brown, and the mast drops down

    From sycamore, oak, and beech ;

And the shadows glide by the horseman's side,

    And death is the goal they reach.

[As he sings the last line, ABADDON emerges from the forest, in
    the guise of a Pedlar, gaily attired, with a cock's plume in
    his hat, and carrying a smart pack.]

FORTUNATUS.

Who may you be ?

ABADDON.

I am the *Pride of Life.*

FORTUNATUS.

The devil you are !

ABADDON.

    The Devil I am, that's certain,

Though you will not believe it, since 'tis true.

FORTUNATUS.

What has become of Mephistopheles ?

ABADDON.

Retired—'twas time—on an annuity,
Invested in a publishing-house that issues
Sceptical volumes of philosophy.
Not a bad trade, withal not good enough
For a brisk age like this, and so I took
His business over, paying a percentage
Upon my earnings.   Lucifer grows old,
And does not understand the Modern Spirit ;
Now, sir, you see I do.

FORTUNATUS.

        You are a humourist.

ABADDON.

So would you be, were you the *Pride of Life*,
And not its dupe.   I have nothing here for *you*.
Still, look upon my shrewd time-serving things.

[He opens his pack.]

Corsets and laces wherewith burgeoning maids
Make themselves buxom of a market-day
For reeking hinds : kerchiefs, and collars, and cuffs,
With gaudy garters for their dimpled knees,

Dimpled with sitting upon Sunday stiles,
Or Monday scrubbings.   Do they what they will,
Their thoughts are on my satchel.   Lord ! how many,
As we stand here, are longing for this lace,
Venetian point—at least I tell 'em so—
And practise, or permit, some twilight theft,
To flaunt this flimsy finery.   It is worth
A library of doubt, and makes more converts
Than all the Encyclopædists.

FORTUNATUS.

                    But why here,
In this remote afforested expanse,
With haply now a hamlet, now a farm,
Surely too desert to be worth the damning,
Bear you your pack ?   Why not in denizened towns,
Where mortals are as thick as trees are here ?

ABADDON.

Sometimes I visit them, but not for that.
Towns can be trusted to corrupt themselves,
My unpaid partners, and my journeys thither
Are taken when my stock-in-trade runs low
And needs replenishing.   These simpering curls,

When duly dangling on a pleated throat,
Will move as many sheep's-eyes, many sighs,
As the most real ringlets ; and no rose
Born of the wind, engendered of the snow,
Or blushingly begotten, can provoke
Homage more hot than this vermilion
Packed in a pouncet-box.

> [He holds up more things.]

      Sachets and scents
To render lasses sweet as lavender,
When comes the time to lay it 'twixt the sheets
And perfume dreaming.   'Tis right pleasant work,
They are cogged so easily.

FORTUNATUS.

     You have books, I see.

ABADDON.

Yes, but the newest and the lightest only,
Leavened with pictures.   Lucifer begged hard
I would take over all his stock-in-trade
Of sceptical polemics.   I refused ;
It has grown so monstrous musty.

FORTUNATUS.

Have you poems?

ABADDON.

No, poems are too visionary for
A realistic world, which much prefers
Cuddling in downright prose.   Good Lord! what stuff!
By women mostly, sage for simpletons,
With rue to follow.

Pick among my pretty things,
Bracelets and betrothal rings,
Kerchiefs with embroidered hem,
Newest scents to perfume them,
Good stout hose and supple garters,
Flasks of home-made elder-waters,
Sovran for a freckled skin;
Drugs to make you plump or thin;
Chemisettes with sleeves and cuffs,
Samples of the latest stuffs
Out of which to fashion gowns
Such as ladies wear in towns;
Combs, and ribbons, and brocades,
Merry thoughts for moping maids;

Ear-rings for your little ears,
Everything you want, my dears,
Everything except a lover,
Who around you soon will hover,
So you buy my pretty things,
Bracelets and betrothal rings.

FORTUNATUS.

But have you nothing for the lads to buy?

ABADDON.

Only some men are producers, that's certain. But all women consume, and can no more withstand gay gear than men can resist winsome faces. Have the right bait, and the fish will soon follow. Once the women are on your side, the game's won. Lucifer knew that, when he was young, and plied Eve with the sweet pulp of an untasted fruit, not Adam with the hard hollow husk of Free Will and Fate. Now he's in his dotage, he argues in the Reviews. Having reasoned so long, he now understands nothing.

FORTUNATUS.

But is it fair to fool the fairest fair,
And make a market of maids' weaknesses?

ABADDON.

Well, I'll tell you a secret; only mind you bury it
in that part of your memory where gratitude resides.
Women are not damned : only a few at least, those
who mountebank man, and so accompany him, for his
worst punishment, to the hell hereafter. Decoy-ducks
are not put in the larder.

FORTUNATUS.

Then, whither do they fare them when they die?

ABADDON.

I would that you could tell me. I have long
Been trying to find out, but fruitlessly.

> *Haply prisoned in the air,*
> *Earth, or sea, or everywhere.*
> *In the violet's steadfast gaze,*
> *Windings of the woodland ways,*
> *In the Springtime's songs and scent;*
> *And the Summer's blandishment.*
> *Lurk they in the lisping corn?*
> *Breathe they in the breaking morn,*
> *Wander with the elusive billow,*
> *Wave in tresses of the willow,*

Flutter upward with the lark,
Drench us in the dewy dark?
Live they in the falling leaves,
Droning gusts and dripping eaves,
Lonely fireside's flickering glow,
Twilight dreams of Long-ago,
Flash of sails upon the sea,
Mirage of felicity?

I call that a right cunning song, and I used to sell it by the gross.   Now they won't look at it,

FORTUNATUS.

There never was a time when simplest maid
Dimpled her pillow with a wanton dream,
Slumbering on such a guileless melody.
Tears from the heart, pure tears from purest well,
Love's virgin disillusion, chance might flow
The faster for that ditty; but, believe me,
There's no damnation in a song like that.

ABADDON.

Who can say?   Damnation has many doors; and the Ivory Gate attracts many whom golden portals

would alarm, and those of brass disgust.   But 'tis a
plausible song.   I wonder who wrote it.

FORTUNATUS.

One whom I knew in youth, fantastic swain,
To whom this passionless panorama, Life,
Appeared a throbbing wonder-world.

ABADDON.

       In flesh
Abides he still?

FORTUNATUS.

     He went behind the scene,
And scanned the paint and pulleys.   Caring not
To live as actor or as audience then,
He waiteth for the dropping of the curtain.

ABADDON.

A Pessimist?   His doom concerns me not.
He is damned already.

FORTUNATUS.

      I have cast a shoe.
Know you a farrier in these sylvan wastes
Can furnish me another?

ABADDON.

No.   But stay.
Franklin the woodreeve hammers out his own,
Vulcan no less than each symbolic god
That stands for mortal mastery.   There's nothing
In the wide range of man's necessity—
Mark you, I say necessity alone—
Not wrought by Franklin and Urania.

FORTUNATUS.

Who is Urania?

ABADDON.

She is his daughter, sir ;
The pair the very wisest twain on earth.
My empire ceases at their rustic gate,
Arrested by their wisdom, faithful watch-dog
That scares all nether vagabonds, and keeps
Their unlocked lives secure from larceny.
Sometimes upon their wicket do I lean,
What time Urania's roses, damask-red,
Flecked with Madonna lilies, are ablow,
And wonder why their secret, plain as June,
Remains their own.

FORTUNATUS.

What is their secret, 'sooth?

ABADDON.

That would be telling.   Go, and find it out;
Though odds are, you will miss it, like the rest.
My trade is not in jeopardy, though they,
Could they convert Archbishops to their creed,
Would make me bankrupt.

FORTUNATUS.

What, then, do they do?

ABADDON.

He tends the kine; Urania brims the pail,
Coaxing the udders with her lissom fingers,
Sweet as the milk they drain.   She skims the cream,
And, with her sleeves tucked up, and white round arms,
Tipped at the elbow with a rosy bud,
Makes the churn sing like boulder-baffled stream.
He threshes out the wheat; she strains the barm,
Kneading and baking cottage loaves that smell
Of every homely virtue.   When he rives
The rough sere remnants of the fallen thorn,

A wimple on her head, and kirtled short,
She pegs the snow-white linen in the wind,
And, singing back her way into the threshold,
Compounds the custard, or with nimble hands
Shells the first pods of summer, dainty-white
In bleachëd tucker, modest pinafore,
A heavenly earthliness.

FORTUNATUS.

            How know you this,
Prohibited her door?

ABADDON.

          Forbidden?   No;
Only, still foiled.   I enter when I will,
But with her florid voice Urania flouts
The pick of all my pack.   Times, she will buy,
But not for show, only for usefulness:
And yet her choice hath more of fancy in it,
More taste, discrimination, true conceit,
Than vanity bestows on simpletons.
She hath no littleness, no passions neither,
Only majestic motions of the mind,
Steered by a steadfast heart.   His daughter, sir,

His very daughter, daughter of his loins,
His love, his wisdom.

FORTUNATUS.

Is he very wise?

ABADDON.

He is strong and gentle.   Who is that, is all.

FORTUNATUS.

You, for the Devil that you boast to be,
Seem much in love with comeliness and virtue.

ABADDON.

To know and reverence Good, and yet do evil,
Is the infernal penalty of the Past.

FORTUNATUS.

That's true.

ABADDON.

It is, of Devil and man alike.
Well, after all, we are brothers.   Plague on your
    megrims!
You have half infected *me* with Pessimism.

Even the Devil has his dark hours, though living
With power to laugh and injure is merry work.
My world's not coming to an end as yet,
While such as you inhabit it, good Duke !

[He shoulders his pack.]

FORTUNATUS.

You know me, then ?

ABADDON.

                    The Devil is too well-bred,
Not to know all the Peerage.   Farther on,
The track divides to narrow and to broad.
The narrow leads you to Urania.
Upon that saddle sits the pride of life,   .
Upon that brow, that manhood, and that title.
I can afford to take a holiday.

[He lifts his hat.]

Life to your Grace, my noble emissary !
She loiters in the garden.   Fare you well !
Get a new shoe. · 'Tis sure to carry you home,
And bring you back again.

[He plunges into the forest, humming as he does so :]

When, with accidental feet,
Wickedness and Wisdom meet,

D

Which of them will win the day ?
Here and there a tress of gray,
Shimmering through the chestnut hair
Over temples tight and spare,
Shows like virtue, making thus
Lingering youth more dangerous.
Ribbons, perfumes, and brocades,
Satins of all sorts and shades,
Buckles of the finest paste,
Toys to jingle from the waist,
Coral necklace, amber stud,—
What are these to flesh and blood,
Fusing, with refined pretence,
Courtesy, concupiscence,
Birth, and bearing, and all that,
For a feather in your hat ?

FORTUNATUS (*alone*).

A wise and witty vagrant.   I forgot me,
Following the deep dark windings of his mirth,
To pay my footing.
                    [Taking out his purse.]
                        Even the Devil, they say,
Should have his due.   What ho !

A VOICE.

What ho !

FORTUNATUS.

See here !

A VOICE.

See here !

FORTUNATUS.

Ridiculous ! I have lost his trail.
It seems as if the forest had a voice.
Into the hollow of some pollard hornbeam
He hath shrunk, and screens him.   'Tis another prank
Whereby he dupes the sadness of existence
With spurious foolery . . . What ho !

A VOICE.

What ho !

FORTUNATUS.

Perhaps he was right.   The Devil is an echo
Of search unsatisfied.

SCENE IV

[FORTUNATUS reaches the rustic gate of URANIA's garden, and dismounts. He hears a voice singing.]

I

The young rooks caw in the elm-tree tops ;
  Dip, yaffel, dip from tree to tree :
The eggs are warm in the hazel copse,
And warm is the lamb that the meek ewe drops ; .
  Dip, yaffel, dip from tree to tree.

II

The bees hang down from the columbine cells ;
  Sing, yaffel, sing from tree to tree :
The throat of the nightingale sinks and swells,
And the wise fool shaketh his cap and bells ;
  Sing, yaffel, sing from tree to tree.

III

The stiff wain creaks 'neath the nodding wheat ;
  Flit, yaffel, flit from tree to tree.
The babe is hushed on its mother's teat,
And the acorn drops at your dreaming feet ;
  Flit, yaffel, flit from tree to tree.

IV

The whimpering winds have lost their way ;
*   Scream, yaffel, scream from tree to tree.*
The trunks stand grim and the fields stretch gray,
And the year that is dead, is dead for aye.
*   Scream, yaffel, scream from tree to tree.*

FORTUNATUS.

How sovranly she sings, as though her voice
Had taken the ether captive, and the air
Lived on the linked enchantment of her tones.
Like to a covert nightingale she nests,
Continuously carolling unseen,
Whileas one halts to hearken. All the place
Seems magical with music, and there is
A bland and delicate texture in the air,
Which the unsounding shuttle of the winds
Hath woven into velvet.

A VOICE (*singing*).

But the rook, and the bee, and the granaried corn,
*   Laugh, yaffel, laugh from tree to tree.*

[URANIA appears before him, in the garden walk, as he stands
by his horse's head.]

FORTUNATUS.

O, pray, sing on !

Like to the afternoon, I paused to listen,
Suspended eavesdropper,—praying to be pardoned.

URANIA.

No need for pardon ; all good things belong
To those that find them good, and you repay
Your pleasure with your presence.

FORTUNATUS.

Then your home

Belongs to me in fee, for have I never
Felt anything so fair.

URANIA.

Conceive it yours,

Yet not in fee, for none of us possess
More than the lease and usufruct of life,
Which is enough ; too many think, too much,
Craving for more.

FORTUNATUS.

My horse had cast a shoe,

And in the forest met I one who said

I haply might replace it by the favour
Of those that dwell herein ; a merry fellow,
Who entertained me with capricious jests
And rhyming raillery.   He only needed
The cap and bells you sang of silverly,
To seem a mummer of the younger days,
With just the russet of our mournful time,
To sober the old habit of his mirth.

URANIA.

It must have been Abaddon.

FORTUNATUS.

         That is a name
Which in the lumber-room of memory fills
Some undiscovered place ; by himself christened
The Pride of Life.

URANIA.

A pedlar ?

FORTUNATUS.

         Yes, the same.
He moved so blithely 'mong the primroses,
The cuckoo's gibe, the wildwood pleasantness,

And melted into leafage so alert,
I could have deemed him dryad had his flouts
Not proved him alien to simplicity.

URANIA.

My father is afield, but shortly will
Call the kine home, and then will serve your need.
The stable lies behind ; give me your horse.
Regale yourself with flowers till I return ;
For May hath quickened a hundred into life,
That yesterday were dreaming.

[URANIA leads his horse away.]

FORTUNATUS (*alone*).

What an equerry !
She placed her hand upon the bridle rein
With such a gentle empery, I could
Not help depute my duty to her will.
Right was the pedlar ; never have I seen
That which we know, and that for which we crave,
In visible perfection thus annealed :
Nature still showing through the enamelled grace
That surfaces the woman.   But there lurks
Deception somewhere to befool the sense

For further disillusion.   Of all shows
In this phenomenal fantastic world,
The slippery, fugitive, elusive stuff
From which imagination loves to weave
Its gossamer affections, there is none
So unsubstantial as a woman's seeming.
She can deceive, when man deceives no more ;
A mirage in the desert, desert proved
By fatuous fancy thousand times bewrayed,
Life's earliest, latest, longest-lingering cheat ;
Persistent in Appearance ; when approached,
A nimbused nothingness.

[URANIA re-enters the garden.]

URANIA.

> Like you my garden ?

FORTUNATUS.

It hath revoked the forfeit of the Fall ;
'Tis Paradise regained.

URANIA.

> The early roses,

Pinched by pernicious visitings of March,
This year will blossom tardily.   But crown-imperials

Encouraged by the dry, undripping Spring,
Have thrust their tasselled canopies aloft
Before their feast is due.   Do you not find
Nature's unpunctuality retrieves
Our too precise forebodings, filling up
All disappointing vacancies with gifts
Not reckoned in our calendar?

FORTUNATUS.

You must

Have rare and expert gardeners, to salute
Maytime with such a rivalry of flowers.

URANIA.

My gardener curtsies to you.   I am he.

FORTUNATUS.

I have seen terraces and trim parterres,
Long-winding walks and trellises festooned,
With gaudy pleasances, but none like this.
What is your secret?

URANIA.

I have no secret, sir,

Save loving be a secret.   Skill have I none,

Save such as tender observation lends,
And wage which these irregularly pay
With most usurious interest, when they smile.
Here are no curious blooms, but simply those
With which the homely cottager arrays
His narrow plot, filched from the roadway side ;
Sweet-smelling stocks, last year not thrown away,
With double-rocket, limber columbine,
Frank rustic oxslips freckled by the sun,
Not like auriculas with powdered faces,
Too careful of their seeming.

FORTUNATUS.

                            How they mingle,
Lilac with peach-blossom, guelder-roses white
With saffron dust of bronze-leafed barbary.
Your garden is an orchard, and your herbs,
From pansies undistinguishable, share
The company of flowers.

URANIA.

                            Kind Nature loves
Concord, not contrast.   It is man divides

With observation too fragmentary,
Her universal purpose.

FORTUNATUS.

What are these?

URANIA.

These are day-lilies, ignorant of the night,
But making by succession swift amends
For their ephemeral sojourn.   Have you not
A garden of your own?   Will you not sit?
[They sit on a rustic bench.]

FORTUNATUS.

A garden have I, but 'tis scarcely mine,
More than the sceptre to a King belongs
Who reigns but doth not govern.   Mine it were,
Could wage but make it so.   But yours seems yours
By some inherent tenure.

URANIA.

Is yours large?

FORTUNATUS.

Not large to look on.

URANIA.

           But too large to love,
Too large to tend?   Each accidental bloom
Is rooted in my heart, lives in my gaze,
And for a helpmate hath the nursing hand.

FORTUNATUS.

Sometimes in loitering vacancy of mood
I pick the wilted roses from their stalk,
Or shrivelled bells of the campanulas.
For that, my hand may serve.   Mefears its touch
Hath no creation in it, and my heart
Would prove an arid soil for such fair plants
As prosper in your moist fresh territory.

URANIA.

You do not love your garden.

FORTUNATUS.

           What is love?

URANIA.

'Tis observation, patience, vigilance,
And infinite indulgence.   Love is wisdom

In tender operation ; having no rights,
But, though a spendthrift, hourly growing richer
By unusurious giving.

FORTUNATUS.

Where learned you that ?

URANIA.

I learned it in my garden, in my home,
And somewhat in my heart ; experience training
The shoots of instinct.

FORTUNATUS.

Love you but your garden ?

URANIA.

Should we not love whate'er is lovable ?
Beauty because 'tis beautiful, and sadness
Because 'tis sad, and sorrow most of all ?
The wrinkled leaves of Autumn are as dear
As Spring's predicting blossoms, so the heart
Demands no payment for its lavishness.
Yet doth my garden teach me Love gets back
More than it hath capacity to give.

Look on it now! the churlishness of Winter
Forgiven and forgotten.

FORTUNATUS.

               Winter reverts,
And the amenable tendrils that absorb
Your fondling fingers will return you then
Callous oblivion.

URANIA.

          Not, if I remember,
Remember and await. They will renew
Their incense and thanksgiving once again.
Love never is lost.

FORTUNATUS.

         Not lost! I ne'er have found it.
Man, shackled to his shadow, cannot move
Without the base companionship of self;
And Love, colossal egotist, would drag
The whole world after it, to reach some goal
Which with the winning vanishes. Desire
Is death in gay disguise, and ravenous nature
Feeds on our fond affections when they slacken.

[A voice is heard singing.]

If you love me, if you love me,
Stay in Heaven, and shine above me,
Stooping not to where we cherish
Yearnings that but pale and perish;
But make longing fond and fonder
For the unreachable Up-yonder.

FORTUNATUS.

Surely it is a childish voice that sings,
Although the words and melody be born
Of mature melancholy?

URANIA.

It is April,
My callow April, canticles aloud,
With throat as blithe and ignorant as the lark's,
Sad rhymes I sometimes murmur to myself
To make me happier.

FORTUNATUS

Who may April be?

URANIA.

Gift of the woods, a fosterling of Spring.
A thrush was singing in a silvery thorn,
Striving to silence every note but his.
But over him the fleeting cuckoo called,
Unchecked and unashamed, and in the thicket,
Where leaves as yet were sparse, a nightingale
Fluted aloud, but unobtrusively.
Primrose and windflower carpeted the ground,
And, in an open space the woodlanders
·Had lately cleared, lay April all alone,
A mould of waxen dimples, still unweaned,
Feeding its fancy with one chubby hand,
Its blue eyes gazing up at the blue sky,
And over its unwondering face a look
Of half-awake half-slumberous content.

FORTUNATUS.

Where was its mother?

URANIA.

                    Nowhere to be found,
Though I outcalled the cuckoo :—cuckoo, sooth,

E

That left this hazard egg within our nest,

[APRIL comes running up the garden-walk.]

Now hatched to what you see.

APRIL.

Urania, a swarm! a virgin swarm!
A swarm of bees upon the midmost bough
Of grand-dad's favourite apple-tree, Northern Spy ;
As thick, as thick, as thick as are the blossoms.

[APRIL claps her hands.]

A swarm in May, a swarm in May,
Is worth a waggon-load of hay.

URANIA.

Nay, curtsey to this courteous gentleman,
And tell him who you are.

APRIL.

I am April, sir.

FORTUNATUS.

Indeed you are.   Then give me April's greeting,
Kissing old Winter ere he takes farewell.

APRIL.

You are not Winter; you are more like Summer.
Why should you go? You go because I come.
See, I will flit away again, and leave
You and my sister-mother to your talk.
Grand-dad can take the swarm.

FORTUNATUS.

Nay, do not go;
And if you stay I will petition leave
To linger still.

URANIA.

We pray you.

FORTUNATUS (*to* APRIL).

When I go,
I would behind me you were pillioned,
Where Care is said to sit.

APRIL.

I will be careful.

FORTUNATUS.

She knows no other meaning of the word.
O happy carelessness!

URANIA.

Now to the swarm.
Fetch you a cloth to spread upon the grass,
And pluck the beanstalk that is most in flower,
And I will bring the ladder and the hive.

APRIL.

And don't forget the sugar and the ale.

FORTUNATUS (*alone*).

I did not think that in this agëd world
There lingered so much youthful happiness.
Is it because these joys themselves are young,
That still they please ; while pleasures late conceived
Affect us feebly even from their birth?

[URANIA and APRIL return.]

APRIL (*to* FORTUNATUS).

Will you not take the swarm?

FORTUNATUS.

I know not how.

APRIL.

Urania will teach you.

[While URANIA prepares to take the swarm, APRIL recites.]

When the bees begin to swarm,
Would you house them well and warm,
Make them fill up comb and cell,
Daub the hive with hydromel,
And around it and between
Sweep the blossom of the bean.
Smear, and you will need no veil,
Face and arms with sweetened ale.
Rub fresh elder-leaves along
Branches near to where they throng.
Poise the hive, ere they begin
Flight afresh, then shake them in.

[URANIA mounts the ladder with the empty hive.]

APRIL.

They never sting Urania : I believe
They'd swarm within the hollow of her hand,
Or hive within her apron, if she bade them.

FORTUNATUS (*aside*).

She limes them with her sweetness, and they hover
Harmless about her head as though she were
Queen-Mother of the cluster.

APRIL.

     To her curls
Some drowsy stragglers cling.

FORTUNATUS (*aside*).

     Deeming them anthers
Of honeyed bell-flower swaying in the wind,
As sways the branch she leans on.

URANIA (*descending with the hive, and placing it*
on the cloth on the grass).

      There ! it is done.
The Queen is safe within, and loiterers will
Rejoin their comrades ere the evening star
Summon the golden drones of crowded heaven
To swarm upon the night. Now, April, say
Those other lines you know about the bees.

APRIL (*reciting*).

A swarm in May, a swarm in May,
Is worth a waggon-load of hay.
For then they sip the nectared wine
That wells within the columbine,

Wake drouthy with the dawn and drink
The dewy spices of the pink,
Into the tulip's chalice dive
To filch its vintage for their hive,
And carry hence, as off they flee,
The gold-dust of the barbary.
Around the foxglove's silent bells
Their mid-day music swerves and swells:
As the frail-folded leaves unclose,
They suck the sweetness of the rose;
Unto the lily-stamens cling
With honeyed feet and pollened wing,
From fields of swaying clover steal
Delicious draught and sugared meal,
And mix, from every tasselled tree,
The mortar for their masonry.

FORTUNATUS.

Where did you learn these seasonable rhymes?

APRIL.

I learned them from Urania—

[Kissing URANIA's hand.]

Did I not?

URANIA.

Stay, dear, and entertain this gentleman,
Till I return !

[URANIA leaves them.]

FORTUNATUS.

Do you know many rhymes ?

APRIL.

Yes, for Urania says verse sheds the husk
And is the core of everything that's good.
You also know some poetry by heart,
Do you not, sir ?

FORTUNATUS.

Once on a time I did ;
And there is music mastered in the years
When I was young as you, that lingers still
In intervals of memory.

APRIL.

Say it me.
Tell me a tale.   May I sit on your knee,
Or shall I tire you ?

FORTUNATUS.

Nay, sweet April maid,

Perch here.

[Lifting her on to his knee.]

Perch there for ever !   Shall the tale

Be in verse or prose?

APRIL.

In verse, of course ; unless

You like prose better.

FORTUNATUS.

I remember none

That is not sad.

APRIL.

Sad songs sometimes are sweet.

FORTUNATUS.

Once on a time a goodly knight,
    And a most lovely lady,
Roamed hand in hand, as children might,
    In alleys green and shady :
There was nothing save themselves in sight,
    And June was in its heyday.

When suddenly from out the wood
   There rushed forth fierce banditti;
And, though she wept, and he withstood,
   They slew him without pity,
And left her to her drearihood,
   To wail this woeful ditty.

"O never when the buds from Spring
   A magic freshness borrow,
Make love your lord or joy your king,
   Forgetful of to-morrow,
Or you will rue the hour and wring
   Your hands in endless sorrow."

APRIL.

Is there no more?   It should not end like that.

FORTUNATUS.

Alas! sweet! endless sorrow is the end.
Nothing comes after that.

APRIL.

          You make me weep.

FORTUNATUS.

As April should sometimes.

APRIL.

But I had rather
The knight had slain the bandits and espoused
His lady-love for ever.

FORTUNATUS (*absently*).

Think it so,
Then so it was ; for mind has mastery
Over the past and future. 'Tis the present
Embarrasses the fancy. . . . But, forgive me. . . .
I know another tale, if not so brief,
Yet somewhat happier.

APRIL.

O, then, tell it me.
I love the long ones, when they end in joy.

FORTUNATUS.

There was a King in olden days,
   With black heart, scowling forehead.
The mighty trembled at his gaze,
   And his sceptre was abhorrëd.

Alike to burgher ånd to boor
  His grasp was hard and greedy :
He had no pity for the poor,
  Indulgence for the needy.

Beside him sate a gentle Queen,
  Compassionate and holy,
Who fed the hungry, clad the mean,
  And comforted the lowly.

Till with hot words he her forbade
  To visit, cheer, or aid them.
Then meekly, though her heart was sad,
  She listened, and obeyed them.

It happed, one day, in hovel rude
  A leper lay a-dying ;
And there was none to take him food,
  And none to soothe his sighing.

Forgetting all, with bread and meat
  She filled a little wallet,
And, sallying out into the street,
  Made haste to reach his pallet.

When lo ! the King, with courtiers girt,
　　Came riding through the city.
The Queen in terror raised her skirt,
　　To screen her work of pity.

Seeing her shrink and bow her head,
　　His brow begun to pucker :
" Now show me what it is," he said,
　　" You hide below your tucker."

She spoke not, but uncovered it ;
　　And look what it discloses !
Not wheaten loaf and dainty bit,
　　But myrtles, pinks, and roses.

" What gauds are these ? " he fumed and cried,
　　" And wherefore were they hidden ? "
" I disobeyed you," she replied,
　　" And trembled to be chidden.

" Food was I taking where, ah me !
　　A lonely leper cowers ;
But the Lord Jesus, as you see,
　　Hath changed them into flowers.

The King dismounted from his horse,
   First smelt pink, rose, and myrtle,
Then knelt, and, smitten with remorse,
   Kissed her white hands and kirtle.

Henceforth he held no sumptuous state
   In courtyard, hall, or stable ;
The poor were welcomed at his gate,
   The hungry at his table.

When died his Queen, and in the tomb
   Was laid with pomp and wailing,
Myrtle at once began to bloom,
   And climb round slab and railing.

And even when the snow lies white,
   And frosty stars are shining,
Clove pinks about her grave are bright,
   And round it roses twining.

APRIL.

And are the roses blooming there to-day ?
How I should like to see them !

FORTUNATUS.

I am told
They clamber there no longer, since men came
Who disbelieved the story : so, they died.
What faith creates, doubt kills.

APRIL.

So grand-dad says ;
And all he says is true.   Would you not like
To see his study, full of learnëd books ?
Grand-dad knows everything.

[They enter, hand-in-hand.   FORTUNATUS scans the book-
shelves, filled with the works of the poets, sages, and
historians of all ages.]

FORTUNATUS.

And does he read them all ?

APRIL.

Yes, all, and then
Explains them to Urania ; those, I mean,
She does not understand without his help ;
And some day he will do the same for me.
You—you can read them all, for you are a man ?

FORTUNATUS.

Once on a time, I understood them better
Than haply now. . . . (*Aside*) One's little learning
    rusts
With the disuse of life ; whereas this man
Has annalists and poets of all time
For comrades and familiars of his leisure,
Yet girds a leathern apron round his loins
To play the farrier to my helplessness. . . .
Where is the stable ?

APRIL.

I will show it you.

[On reaching the stable, they find FRANKLIN shoeing the horse,
and URANIA holding up the horse's hoof.]

FORTUNATUS.

Nay, you confound me with your useful grace,
And stooping dignity.   I pray you, let—me !

URANIA.

See, it is done.   Now, April, to the larder !

[URANIA and APRIL quit them, and FRANKLIN conducts
FORTUNATUS back to the garden.]

FRANKLIN.

There is no office in this needful world
But dignifies the doer, if done well;
And she brings dignity to all she does,
Lending her mind and hand, whenever wanted.
My part shows feebler; for, although 'twill serve,
The shoe is but a makeshift.

FORTUNATUS.

        Did I stand
Stammering my thanks until the day was done,
I still should be your debtor.   Thank you! thank
    you!

FRANKLIN.

Nay, then repay us with your company,
And share the meal we take when evening strews
The quiet of long shadows on the grass,
And friendly converse satisfies like prayer.
I will rejoin you shortly.

FORTUNATUS (*alone*).

        What man is this,
Who unto brawny and bucolic thews,

F

Rustic complexion, sweating craftsmanship,
And yokel's occupation, joins a port
Of simple elevation, now alas !
In court and palace well-nigh moribund ;
Who does a smithy's work with kingly hands,
And from the lowliest labour glances up
With brow of meditation ?   Opposites,
Within this hospitable calm abode,
By some strange craft are amicably wed,
And life's rude contradictions reconciled.
For such a sire to engender such a daughter,
Congenitally noble, gentle, wise,
Is within nature's narrow competence.
But whence came such a stock ?   And is it choice,
Or some felicitous fortuity,
Planted them here ?

[FORTUNATUS remains in meditation till he sees FRANKLIN
returning.]

Hither he wends, his work-day garb foregone,
Wearing the aspect of that goodliest thing
Matured by time, an English gentleman.

[FRANKLIN leads FORTUNATUS to a spot in the garden where
URANIA and APRIL have prepared supper.]

FRANKLIN.

How grateful, when the functions of the day
Finish their cheerful course, to sit within
The waving curtain of this leafy lime,
And eat the bread, and drink the draught, that's
    earned.

FORTUNATUS.

I have earned neither, though you give me both,
And come an idle vagrant to your board.

FRANKLIN.

Nay, you have ridden from far, and exercise
Is one of leisure's worthiest offices.
Do you not find the canopy of heaven
And carpet of the ground a richer room,
More varied and luxurious to the sense,
Than circumscribing wall and stagnant roof?

FORTUNATUS.

In such an hour as this. But rarely is it,
In our capricious ether, we can live
As free and unconditioned as to-day.

FRANKLIN.

Do you not think we quarrel overmuch
With the conditions that we cannot change?
The seasons are not ours to rule, and hence
Unto their fitful government the wise
Accommodate their senses.

FORTUNATUS.

                But is will
So sure an anæsthetic it can blunt
The alertness of the nerves to heat and cold,
And make them face mercurial temperature
As though it stood for ever at fixed fair?

FRANKLIN.

Will leagued with action, yes.   While opulent ease
Cowers from the sleety hurricane and warms
Its passive pulses by the velvet hearth,
See poor laborious lowliness, though clad   ,
In floating flimsiness and wetly shod,
But every sinew braced to use, extort
From steely wind and parsimonious frost
A comfortable glow and tingling warmth.
'Tis not the seasons that have changed, but we.

The poets who of old extolled the Spring
Minded no more the blustering sheen of March
Than do the windflowers or the primroses.
Not overfed, nor overclad, nor drugged
To counteract gross surfeiting, they felt
Gust, cloud, or shower, as little as the lambs:
We fill up crack and cranny, and ensconce
In snug alcove our padded limbs, and then
Rail at the heavens for using wrongfully
Our artificial senses.

FORTUNATUS.

You should blame,
Not man, but Fate, which stimulates the mind
To invent the arts that undermine the body.
The dupe and victim of his faculties,
Man lies on the soft couch himself hath made,
Proud of his enervating power, and christens
With the fond name of Progress each new link
Enslaving him to matter.

FRANKLIN.

Who shall say
If the wind drives the cloud, or cloud the wind?

But long as man feels consciousness of choice,
Essential or fantastic, let man choose.
We feed not on the poisons we discover,
Nor fall upon the sword our wit hath sharpened.
Why then should man to matter fall a slave,
Being first so much its master that it yields
Its secrets to his seeking, nor reject
Its less ennobling aid and services?
Let man do all things, but remain himself,
And, 'mid progressive splendour, still maintain
The lordly rule of simple appetite.

[URANIA beckons to APRIL, and they retire.]

FORTUNATUS.

Was it by choice or accident you fixed
Your home in this delectable retreat?
And, having proved it, are you well content
With your aloof and narrow territory?

FRANKLIN.

Life is as large as we ourselves do make it.
But little room is needed for the scope
Of individual faculty, desire,
And practicable duty.   If we fill

More space than nature hath allotted us,
We waste ourselves in tenuous expansion,
And all our force but drifts to feebleness.

FORTUNATUS.

And are you happy?

FRANKLIN.

      ·Yes, if happiness
Be to have little, but to want no more,
And know, withal, this little is the sum
Of all worth having.   Work, Love, Nature, Art,
From these the sane intelligence constructs
The four-walled citadel wherein it dwells
Impregnable to Fate.

FORTUNATUS.

      But not to Death!
Patient besieger who invests us all,
And starves all out at length.

FRANKLIN.

      Yet not to him
The fortress is surrendered.   It is held
By all the wise and brave whose progeny,

Or others by their high example taught,
Retain the key of life, and leave death still
Encamped without.

FORTUNATUS.

Are you then satisfied
To bid farewell to Work, Love, Nature, Art,
Remitting these to others, while you pass
Into the loveless and unnatural ground,
Where you will work no more, and storied stone
Is Art's last word to you, you will not hear?

FRANKLIN.

There was a time I had a feud with Death.
The hardest lesson wisdom has to learn
Is, having learnt to love and reverence life,
To learn serenely to relinquish it.
We do not purchase life; it is a gift,
Which we are free to forfeit, when we will,
Unto the Unseen Hand that gave it us.
The wise, the brave, retain it as a boon
Until the Giver himself demands it back.
Behold to what a goodly world we come !
For us the spacious bounty of the air,

The impregnable pavilion of heaven,
And silent muster of the disciplined stars.
For us the sun replenished, and for us
The punctual patience of·the lonely moon ;
The planetary seasons moving round
·Their stately soundless orbits, fostering life
In blade, leaf, flower, blossom, and reddening fruit ;
The mountains motionless, the mobile sea,
Freshness of dawn and frankincense of eve,
And vestal hush of meditative night.
Paupers we come into a world prepared
As for some regal guest ; prepared, arrayed,
With temples, shrines, and statues of the gods,
Cathedrals where unfaltering twilight dwells,
Subduing souls to sympathy and prayer :
Lakes, woods, and waterfalls, and cities girt
With walls majestic circling sumptuous tombs
Of sceptres superseded, thrones interred,
Prodigious pageant open to us all.
And if to greet the superficial sense
Of each fresh, eager, welcome visitant,
These splendours are unfolded, think of those,
More precious, immaterial bequests,
Left by the mighty ancestors of thought :

Story and song in many a human tongue
Magnificently sounded, epics pitched
In high heroic key by bards that tuned
Their instruments to chariot wheels enlocked,
Helm-plumes unhorsed, and women wailing round
The wind-blown smoke of crackling funeral pyres.
For us, for all, who hither nothing bring
Save naked insignificance, the choir
Of archangelic poets have composed
Their universal music, stately hymn,
Mellifluous lyric, undulating ode,
And tragedy tremendous steadying life
With awful issues.   Sages, seers, and saints,
Sounders of earth and searchers of the sky,
Heroes and hierophants, have left behind
The testament of science, wisdom, love.
Compared with this inheritance, bequeathed
By all to each, the wisest, worthiest,
And most improving occupant of life,
Can leave but little ; while the barren herd,
Who feed upon the pasture of all time,
Live sleek, lie soft, lament themselves, and die,
Are thankless wastrels.

FORTUNATUS.

From your glowing picture
Life's shadows are omitted ; pain and woe,
Carnage, disease, man's discontent with man,
The instability of love, the blight,
The melancholy mildew, swift or slow,
That blasts the fairest blossoms of the heart,
Pitiful yearning, pitiless denial,
Vast vista leading nowhere !

FRANKLIN.

You forget,
The moon casts darker shadows than the sun
Having less light.   Seen with meridian gaze,
The proud exclusive privilege of grief,
The sovereignty of sorrow throning man
Above the unsentient and the oblivious world,
His disappointments, failures, doubts, regrets,
Ennoble his mortality, and keep
His aspirations humble, tender, quick
To understand and sympathise with weakness.
Let cloudy sorrow gather as it may,
So long as hope, though lowly, doth not set,

Upon the gloomy wrack behold! there shines
The rainbow of man's tears.

FORTUNATUS.

Alas! I fear
These wise reflections comfort but the wise.
The poor, the lowly, who inherit woe,
Yet share not time's magnificent bequests,
In such a rich dispensary will find
Small medicine for their ills.

FRANKLIN.

The poor, the lowly,
Are wiser than our leisured wisdom deems.
Allotted tasks and homely wants secrete
No pessimistic poison. Life is well
Would we leave life alone. 'Tis restless thought,
Having no home nor duties definite,
Hence free to range and raven where it will,
Disturbs weak hearts with vague imaginings.

FORTUNATUS.

Go preach this in the highway, and be stoned.

[URANIA and APRIL return, carrying flowers and an empty
    basket. This they fill with what is left of the meal.]

FRANKLIN.

Into the highway Wisdom wanders not,
But works within the ample territory
Annexed unto its threshold.   Each can do
But little, but if each would do that little, ·
All would be done.   The individual task
Is for the individual life enough,
And, if performed ungrudgingly, absolves
The individual conscience.

FORTUNATUS.

Where go you with your basket and your flowers?
May I ask
Where go you with your basket and your flowers?

FRANKLIN.

There is no lovelier hamlet in the land
Than that to which they wend.   Its antique church,
Perched on the summit of a grassy hill,
Looks down on cottage garden, cottage roof,
Almshouse and school, sawpit, and forge, and inn,
Picture of rustic plenty, health, and peace.

URANIA.

Yet sickness sometimes lifts the humble latch,
And behind woodbined threshold penury lurks,

And ever do we find some pallid hand
Outstretched to hail our coming.

APRIL.

                              And we meet
No wicked King upon the way to change
The food to flowers, and so we carry these
To deck the village chancel, entering through
Its lowly Door of Humility.

FORTUNATUS.

                              Fare you well,
Sweet fosterling of Spring ; and when I come,
If come I may, where blithely you abide,
May I find April always !

    [He lifts her up and kisses her, then turns to URANIA.]

                              Gracious maiden,
Who beautify life's burdens, and ennoble
Life's lowliest offices, I pray you deign
Take my poor homage with my richest thanks.

[He mounts his horse, and rides homeward through the forest.]

I ! I have no more youth than autumn hath,
When time, with useful sickle in his hand,
Bends to his homely reaping.   Love and I

Are all a hot and parching summer apart,
And I await the winter. . . . Never again !
Though well I can recall the sweetness of it :
The moonlight, and the starlight, and the song
Of dewy-throated nightingale—O, I know,
Even as the nightingale itself, each note,
Each glad, sad, sharp, unsatisfying note,
That ripples up the clear ascent of love,
But to subside and sink into itself,
Silent as bare volcano that no more
Surges, yet sleeps not, and still brooding low
In its own hollow entrails, slow consumes
Itself to ashes.   Cheat ! thief ! murderer ! liar !
Thou art the cruellest, bitterest thing in the world,
The poisonous honey in the fleshly flower.
Yet why not cull the flower itself and leave
The poison undistilled ?   Thus do the wise.
Am I a child, I should do otherwise ?
'Tis but a choice of bitters.   But she !   But she ?
O, she hath morning in her gaze, and noon
For garland and for girdle.   Is she fixed,
Deep-rooted in her garden, hedgëd round
Against the wildwood passion of her kind ?
Pluck strongly, and the stalk of prudence snaps.

Savour the sweetness, wear, then fling away. . . .

This is the place that nimble vagabond

Chose for his vanishing. . . . What ho!

A VOICE.

What ho!

FORTUNATUS.

The voice   .

Sounds like an echo, yet not twin to mine.

The answering woodland is transmuting it,

Making it fanciful.

[He rides on, at a foot's pace, and shortly perceives ABADDON
sitting on a stile.]

Ha! there you sit,

As idle as a dial when the sun

Sulks in the clouds.   Have none, then, smiled on you

Since late we parted?   Any one would think

It is the very season made for selling.

ABADDON.

And so it is.   But, apprehend you not,

When misselthrushes flute and maidens quit

The pruning of their roses to attend

A dulcet duke, I trade by deputy.

Hath she not all the heavens in her face,
Yet earth in every footstep?

FORTUNATUS.

                              She is fair
As dewdrops in the morning.

ABADDON.

                              Tell her that,
And I will hang my pack upon a tree,
And whistle through the greenwood, unconcerned,
Your summer pensioner.

FORTUNATUS.

                              And wherefore so?
You would not sell one ribbon more or less,
For love-song of my chanting.

ABADDON.

                              Should I not?
You are not in the trade, so do not know.
All lovers are my partners when they woo:
The partnership's dissolved when once they wed,
And find that marriage is a bankrupt stock.

G

The Pride of Life!   The Pride of Life!

Every maid would be a wife,

For the pretty things Love dangles,

Kisses, compliments, and bangles,

On the road in such profusion,

To the goal of disillusion.

FORTUNATUS.

Who spoke of marriage?   'Tis a musty word.

ABADDON.

Keep yourself fresh, lord duke.   I see you know.

Return and woo Urania in her garden,

When nubile rose and modest mignonette

Scent the white chamber of a maiden's mind

With treacherous ecstasy.   My duty to you.

[He leaps from the stile, and vanishes into the wood singing.]

But again spring music and summer skies,

Sing, yaffel, sing from tree to tree,

Will teach the witless and dupe the wise ;

For love is the sorrow that never dies :

Sing, yaffel, sing from tree to tree.

[FORTUNATUS breaks into a rapid trot, not drawing rein till he
    reaches his own lands, shortly after sunset.   Then, riding
    slowly, he shortly recites aloud.]

FORTUNATUS.

If I again could love, it would be you,
Who to my life both fruit and blossom bring,
Who make the new seem old, the old seem new,
Content my Autumn, and recall my Spring.
With you, if any, it were sweet to share
The tender-torturing tumults of the heart ;
But I the pain of loving cannot bear,
Whose bare remembrance makes old wounds to smart.
For yours to live with mine, your love must die,
Since I am only living with the dead :
Therefore, sweet heart, forgive me if that I
Lay on the pillow of the past my head.
Be love celestial lethe, then Above
Love me, and you shall learn if I can love.

Whence came that far-off sonnet, half true, half false,
Half actual, half fantastic ?   Did it issue
From silent mechanism, inly made
By the contriving Past ?   Let but the Present
Touch the right stop, and straight the tune is played,
In scrannel fashion.   'Tis the first—since when ?
Urania lured that music from the hollow

Of this poor unused instrument.   Urania !
O vowelled name, just linked with consonants,
As in the clustered Canterbury-bell
The threading stalk is smothered by the flowers !

SCENE V

[In URANIA'S chamber.]

APRIL (*sitting up in her crib*).

Was he not kind and gentle?   How I wish
I knew who he is, that I might pray for him,
Adding his name to yours and grandpapa's.
You love him, do you not ?

URANIA.

                    Love is a word
Best kept for home and those high homeless thoughts
We meditate but see not.   I love *you*,
My dear, near April, Father, and my Garden,
The poor, the dead, all that is sad or noble,
Famed or afar.   Between the two extremes
Of close and unattainable there lies
A world of liking, sweet, but not of love.
He is a stranger.

APRIL.

But if he lived with us—
I almost think he would, if grand-dad asked him—
Then you could love him ?

URANIA.

Maybe.   Good-night.   Sleep sound.
We'll talk of that to-morrow.

[She kisses APRIL, who settles herself to sleep, and then walks
to the open window and listens to the nightingales.]

URANIA (*to herself*).

Childhood drowns
The fancies of to-day in rippling slumber,
Waking to-morrow unto fresh affections.
But love, if once matured within the mind,
Is love to-day, to-morrow, and for ever.

APRIL.

Read me to sleep, Urania.   I am wakeful.

[URANIA takes up a volume that lies on a table by the side of
her own bed, opens it, and reads aloud.]

A summons to my slumbering spirit came,
    Whereat I rose and followed.   Then I saw

Star after star, too numberless to name,
  In orderly procession onward draw.

Following the trail of a down-trending moon,
  They chanted to some unseen Hand that played,
Quiring withal so sovranly in tune,
  That silence was the only sound they made.

I fain had into slumber back withdrawn,
  Awed unto dread: when lo! arresting sight!
Rapt in a dream, slow-moving toward the dawn,
  Past me there swept the coroneted Night.

[She sees APRIL has fallen asleep.]

URANIA.

Asleep! how swift she hath been lullabied
By that she understands not! Thus it is.
'Tis the unknown that soothes and folds us round
With its dark curtain. To the known we wake,
To find it inefficient.

[She returns to the open window and again gazes out.]

" *Rapt in a dream, slow-moving toward the dawn.*"
Who wrote that must be noble. But who wrote it?
Again the Unknown, making impossible
All known, ignoble love!

SCENE VI

[The DUKE's library.]

FORTUNATUS (*asleep in a chair, and talking in his sleep*).

Why do you visit me to-night, lost sweet,
With all your golden hair dishevelled to your feet?
I never loved you.   Like a cloud I passed
Over your life, an instant overcast,
Then brilliantly nuptialled.   Now you sleep
Where waves as blue as veins in your white hand
Make silvery music upon golden sand,
And seamews——

Dear little saint, chaste and simple,
Cloistered in a snow-white wimple,
Guarding your rebellious hair,
Come you from the Heaven above me,
Now at last to own you love me?—
Loved me all the while, but dared not
Sanctify the doubts you shared not;
Dying of a wish unspoken,
With a heart—broken—broken—broken.

Love is foolish, Fate is wise :
Back to your grave and Paradise !
Or who knows what yet might be ?
No ! I have forgotten thee.

Medusa-Messalina ! dual-christened,
Yes ! 'twas like that the slim snakes hissed and
     glistened,
When thou, accurst of Wisdom, dragged me prone,
And made my heart as rocky as thine own.
Whence reekest thou, lovely lascivious witch ?—
I lust thee not.   Back to thy nether pitch !

Poor little wilted flower!   Wherefore on me
Settled the fluttering wing of thy affections ?
I froze into myself, but thou would'st follow,
Only to find it hollow—hollow—hollow.
Yet in that sepulchre thou layest warm,
With palpitating heart within a marble arm.
Fond foolish fosterling of barren love,
A stranger to the last, where hast thou gone ?

That does not rhyme.   I once had the trick.
Now I suppose it too has gone—gone with love ?
Why do not love and gone rhyme ?   There is reason

in them, and kinship. Love rhymes with above; yet
they are a universe apart. Love should rhyme with
——Urania! Urania rhymes with nothing. And
yet—— What a misleading thing is verse! Lust
chimes with trust; ay, but with dust also. That's
the proper ending.

> See! they come! . . . tripping, trooping,
> Winged and wanton, swerving, swooping,
> Singly now, and now together,
> Waving torch and tender tether:
> Round me, near me, now retreating,
> Pupils flashing, bosoms beating,
> Lissom limbs and languid bodies,
> Each a momentary goddess!
> You—and you—and you—the last one
> Dissipating every past one!
> These in velvet, those in cotton,
> Fancied, fondled, and forgotten:
> This the fresh, and that the fashion—
> What a carnival of passion!

No! touch me not! I loathe your sterile kisses.
My lips are icicles, that will not melt
To torrid tempters; and my veins are bloodless.

'Twas you—yes, you !—and you !—that drained them
    dry.

Away ! there is no charm nor incantation

In the foul philtres of lubricity

To stir the disillusioned : None of you !

No ! none ! I say ! . . . Urania ! . . . These roses——

        [He slowly wakes.]

Not in her garden !   Yet I deemed I was.

Whose garden was it, then ?   Where am I now ? . . .

Asleep and dreaming in my chair ! . . . To bed !

END OF ACT I

ACT II

SCENE I

URANIA (*singing*).

Now that milch-cows chew the cud,
Everywhere are roses, roses ;
Here a-blow, and there a-bud,
Here in pairs, and there in posies.
Roses from the gable's cliff
With pale flaky petals strowing
All the garden path, as if
Frolic Summer took to snowing.

[There is a knock at the outer door.]

URANIA.

Enter and welcome.   I am too intent

To greet you at the threshold.   Enter, I say.
Nor loaf nor oven will wait ; so pass within.

[ABADDON enters.]

URANIA (*going on with her work*).

The very visitor I wanted.

ABADDON (*aside*).

.   So !

The spell has worked prodigiously.   (*To* URANIA)
      Fair lady,
I in my pack to-day have gauds so deft,
They would make plainness comely, slattern limbs
Natty and trim as Venus when she rose
Up from her rippling pillow on the sea,
Flushed with the rosy daintiness of dawn,
With her own mould for corset, and the fringe
Of wind-blown lace for flounce and furbelow.

[He puts his pack on the table, and opens it.]

Now, look on this cuirass !

URANIA.

                    Please mind my loaves,

[She puts them, one after the other, in the oven.]

I'll heed you presently.

ABADDON (*holding up the cuirass*).

               See ! they who clasp
This firm but frolic jerkin to their waist,
Need be no more beholden unto Nature,
Who is an artist accidentally,
As sooth she was when she imagined You,
But far too often works with niggard hand,
Or else the plastic matter of the flesh
Disposes disproportionately. Now this,
This animated breast, compelling buckler—
Look on them well !—appear as if repoussed
Upon the very lines of Juno's mould,
Its dimpled crevices and swelling curves,
A paragon of rounded sensuousness.

URANIA (*turning round, after having put the last*
loaf in the oven).

And do they wear that lubricating lie,
That fleshless falsehood ! Palpitating maids
Puff themselves out with hollow buxomness,
To lead some breathless gaby at their heels
A scentless paper-chase ! You might as well
Stick candles in the sockets of a skull,
And swear it lives. Pack up your trumpery.

ABADDON.

I thought you wanted me.

URANIA.

And so I did ;
But for the marketing of honest stuff,
To make sweet childhood simpler : something plain,
Rustic, and true, yet best of all its sort,
Nowise inferior, though the sort be scorned
By shoddy splendour.

[He shows her summer stuffs for gowns.]

URANIA (*choosing one of them*).

This comports with her,
And with her frolic limbs will fall and flow,
Her natural drapery.

ABADDON.

Nothing for yourself?
The Duke will come again.

URANIA.

What duke ?

ABADDON.

                              Why, he
That cast a shoe and lingered with you while
The dial darkened onward, nor bethought
To heed the admonition of its shadow.
That was Duke Fortunatus.

URANIA.

                              Was it?   Well?

ABADDON.

Should he return, as verily he will,
Would you not like to look your comeliest?
A duke! a Duke!

URANIA.

                    His name will not behold me,
But he himself; and, should he come again,
Like any other accidental guest,
Will find me what I am.

        [She folds up the material, and pays for it.]
                         Thank you.   And now,
You to your outer work, and I to mine.
Stay, I will fetch a horn of home-brewed ale,
To speed you on your way.

ABADDON (*alone*).

How good they smell,
These household crusts a-baking! Judged by them,
There's not a scent in my distillery,
But savours of the polecat.

[URANIA returns with a horn of ale.]

ABADDON (*having quaffed it*).

My reverence, lady.

[He shoulders his pack and departs. URANIA gives a look at
the loaves in the oven, then examines afresh the stuff
she has bought, gets her scissors, and begins cutting it.]

URANIA.

How like her name my fosterling will look,
Frocked in this pretty stuff! Like apple-blossom
On tender tree not yet allowed to bear
Burden of fruit, its daintiness will show
Fair promise of a ripeness yet to be.
The strange untimely winter of his mind
Melted before the sunniness and song
Of her unclouded nature ; and her heart
Seemed further to expand with his expansion.
I think they loved each other at first sight,

So must I make her comely to his gaze,
To please them both. . . . So he is Duke Fortunatus.
I mind me of the name.   These designations
Are advertised by every common tongue,
Which, seeming thus familiar with the far,
Feign for themselves in turn a false distinction.
He needs no label to be recognised.
Urbanity was in his gait and speech,
By sadness more ennobled.

SCENE II

[As ABADDON reaches the garden gate he meets FORTUNATUS
just dismounting.]

ABADDON.

Good morrow to your Grace.   A goodly day.
Have you so quickly cast another shoe,
Here not a summer month ago?   Mefears
Your farrier is a fumbler.   ʹ

FORTUNATUS.

Pride of Life !
Be that the name by which you still are known.

H

ABADDON.

It is, where I just come from.   But for you
I have another.   *Lust of the Flesh*, we call it.
The Pagan Proteus and the Christian Devil
Are kin, and sooth all Nature's progeny
Are wonderfully like.   Without an alias,
How could I journey through this thankless world
That brands me an impostor, and would fain
Curtail my freedom ?   Hence when Vice awhile
Falls out of fashion, and the chase grows hot,
I fling away my feathers, and appear
In Virtue's vestments grave-caparisoned.
That answers just as well.   For mortal states,
Distorted from their birth, perforce must use
All things awry, and Virtue's very self,
Fooled to the perch and apex of perfection
By my complacency—a trick I have—
Straight   pitches   headlong.   Now, *you* are not
      virtuous,
So need I practise no disguise with you.
Lust of the Flesh—behold me !   She's within,
Baking with alabaster arms the loaves
Of household continence.   She is alone.

In ! in !   And *Pride of Life*, and *Lust of the Flesh*,
Twin names, godfather your prosperity !

[He goes on his way, and FORTUNATUS leads his horse to the
    stable.   As he does so, he hears URANIA singing.]

> *Now that milch-cows chew the cud,*
>   *Everywhere are roses, roses ;*
> *Here a-blow, and there a-bud,*
>   *Here in pairs, and there in posies.*
> *Roses from the gable's cliff*
>   *With pale flaky petals strowing*
> *All the garden-paths, as if*
>   *Frolic Summer took to snowing.*
>
> *Roses crimson, roses white,*
>   *Deadly pale or lively blushing,*
> *Both in love with June at sight ;*
>   *So their maiden blood is rushing*
> *To and fro in hope to hide*
>   *Tumult it but thus discloses.*
> *Bring the Bridegroom to the Bride !*
>   *Everywhere are roses, roses.*

FORTUNATUS.

How sweet is unsophisticated song,
Heard accidentally ; for then the voice,

Having no vain collusion with the ear,
Sounds innocently true.   Sing on ! sing on !
Till there be nothing in the midsummer air
Save You, and roses.

SCENE III

FORTUNATUS.

Over your lintel Greeting is engraved,
And so I enter.

URANIA.

All may enter here,
Who want its inmates.

FORTUNATUS.

And I wanted you,
Be the avowal not too frank,—and April :
April, that plaything of the primroses,
Your blithe unmothered sock-lamb of the Spring,
Who crept into my heart that afternoon,
And warmed its wintriness.

URANIA.

She is happy, haying :
Thinking 'tis she that puts the swathes a-cock,

And piles them on the wain ; her grand-dad's shadow,
As close and as superfluous ; yet, like it,
Gift of the sun himself.   You will find them both
Out in the meadow to the right, beyond
The orchard-gate.

FORTUNATUS.

Will you not come with me ?

URANIA.

When I have done the work I have to do.

FORTUNATUS (*looking at the stuff she has purchased
from* ABADDON).

A woman's work ; right suitable, withal
More timely, is it not, for night than noon ?

URANIA.

You know women's hours, I see, our trysts with time,
And that the needle points to westering day,
And not due south, as now.   Yet 'tis not that
Which keeps me from the hayfield, but this task,

[She opens the oven door.]

A King once did, and did it slovenly,
As I tell April.

FORTUNATUS.

But his thoughts were fixed

On far-off things.

URANIA.

The nearest should be farthest

For uncrowned mortals; and these homely pans

Forbid me go afield.

FORTUNATUS.

What pretty stuff!

You bought it from Abaddon?

URANIA.

Instantly,

To make a frock for April, and he pressed

A thousand things upon me, newly coined

To cog the curious.

FORTUNATUS.

He knows human nature.

URANIA.

Then am I neither natural nor human,

For I bought nothing.

FORTUNATUS.

    This stuff proves you both.

URANIA.

Why are you wise enough to reason thus,
And yet at heart keep wintry? Wisdom lends
Colour and temperature to every season,
Leading the footsteps of subservient time
Which way it will.

FORTUNATUS.

      Unwisely then have I
Followed the slow irreparable days,
Knowing not where nor whither, till they led
My bridle to your porch ; since when, my thoughts
Have journeyed here so often, that my feet
Were forced at length to bear them company.

URANIA.

Timely you come. I want a messenger
To carry to the field the mid-day meal.
'Tis near the stroke, and everything is ready,
The pasties hot, the cider freshly drawn,—
All, save a carrier.

FORTUNATUS.

Then give *me* the basket.

URANIA.

There! shoulder it like that. And, mind, your thoughts
Be on the way not truant to your task.
That very thoughtlessness the thoughtful scorn
In life's meek sumpters, guarantees our loads
Securely to their goal.

FORTUNATUS.

Then will I think
Of nothing but the pasties and the cider,
Unless it be your coming, when your loaves
Turn nut-brown in the baking.

SCENE IV

[The hayfield.]

APRIL.

See, grand-dad, see!
Dinner is coming. Who is it that brings it?

[She runs forward to meet FORTUNATUS.]

O, it is you!   I had begun to think
You had forgotten grand-dad and Urania.

FORTUNATUS (*putting down the basket, lifting her in*
his arms, and kissing her).

And you as well! moist wilding of the woods,
Your absence has been near me all the while.

APRIL.

I am so glad you have come.   But let me help.
It is too heavy for you to carry alone.

FRANKLIN (*approaching them*).

Welcome, once more! and welcome none the less
For what you bring.   You'll share our meal with us?

FORTUNATUS.

Gladly, if April's appetite can spare
A place for yet a third.

[They take their repast together, under a hedgerow; at the end
   of which APRIL runs about, playing, while FORTUNATUS
   and FRANKLIN remain seated.]

FRANKLIN (*taking a volume of " Horace " from the*
bottom of the basket).

The basket was not emptied; one more dish
Lurks at the bottom, scarcely one to tempt

April's untutored palate, doubtless packed
Before Urania knew fair chance had sent
Yet more congenial company than this,
To round the restful hour with.   *

FORTUNATUS.

Read it me.

FRANKLIN.

Nunc mihi res, non me rebus subjungere conor.
[Closing the book.]
Man is the lord, not slave, of circumstance.
If the rich past bequeath him only leisure,
He to that precious legacy should add
The gain of labour; while if labour be
His sole inheritance, he wisely will
Buy leisure with its superfluity.

FORTUNATUS.

Which have *you* done?

FRANKLIN.

The first,—if selfishly,
As sometimes I am hazarded to think,
Since that the burden I evaded falls
On other shoulders.

FORTUNATUS.

Do you then repent you?

FRANKLIN.

No; for that burden, burdensome to me,
To most men seems the lightest load that life
Can lay on mortals, and, if found too heavy,
May be laid down, since rank, wealth, idleness,
Are accidents not substance of our birth,
Mere garments to discard.

FORTUNATUS.

And have you found
In labour yoked with leisure full content?

FRANKLIN.

Yes.　But observe, 'tis chosenly I live,
Not in compulsion; for when growth once adds
Reason to instinct, man must understand
The Universe he lives in and himself,
Or find in Reason only a fresh load,
Badly adjusted.

FORTUNATUS.

How is he to know?

FRANKLIN.

I did not speak of Knowledge.   There are men,
Seem to know all things knowable, withal
Understand nothing ; even as though they had
Circled the earth and yet conceive it flat.
'Tis Understanding that defines the march
Betwixt the wise and foolish.

FORTUNATUS.

                              What is wisdom ?

FRANKLIN.

First to observe What Must Be, and obey it.
Next to discern What May Be, and to choose
Rightly among life's possibilities.
Life is an opportunity ; and hence
It doth behove us never to confound
The real with the specious, but perceive
What is of value, what is valueless.
The rest pertains to Will, which, once convinced,
Convinced, I mean, with sovran certainty,
Perforce must follow Wisdom.   That is all.

FORTUNATUS.

Yes, that is all. 'Tis little, yet 'tis much,
And few possess it. Yet, till seized by all,
Seems it not lack of charity to live
Content with having it?

FRANKLIN.

Not so! Remember
Obedience to What Must Be. No one man,
In the short transit of his single course,
Can hope to sway the millions of mankind.
But he can mould himself, and haply those
Who travel in his orbit, kindred, friends,
Unto them radiating wisdom's warmth,
Rejoiced to share it with them. Why should you,
Because the world is foolish, not be wise?
Not cheerful, should it be perversely sad?
Give wingëd Perseus shelter, Perseus sent
By Pallas' self, and he will not impose
The earth upon your shoulders, far too small
For that intolerable penal task.
Times there have been, and time will be again,
When Fancy offers to diseased mankind

Prompt panaceas, sure phalansteries.

There are none such ; and faith in them begets

First disillusion, then despondency,

With all its pestilent base brood, lame doubt,

Distrust of greatness, disbelief in good,

Divorce betwixt the spirit and the flesh,

Adultery with matter ;—crowning curse,

Abortion of the pregnant boon of life.

To pamper self-complacency, and seem

Yet wearier and more worthless than they are,

The sufferers give their malady a new name,

And call it Pessimism.   The thing is old.

Man's follies all are old, old is the cause,

Old is the remedy.   Walk toward the light,

The shadows fall behind.   Yet do not walk,

Imagining that it never will be night,

But love alike the darkness and the dawn,

And in your heart it always will be noon.

APRIL (*running up to* FRANKLIN).

To work !   To work !   O lazy grand-dad !   See,

Urania comes.   The village clock hath chimed,

And leaves you gossiping still.   It is not I,

This time, that is the truant.

FRANKLIN (*rising*).

Kiss me, sweet,

And I shall work the blither.

APRIL (*to* FORTUNATUS).

You will help?

We want as many hands as we can get ;

For if you cannot take a swarm of bees,

We all can ted the hay.   Why, look at *me* !

[They all join in the haymaking, singing as they do so.]

APRIL *sings*.

When the ladysmocks have faded,
When the lanes are arched and shaded,
When the lambs have lost their fleeces,
When the mid-day heat increases,
When the keen-eyed kestrel hovers
Round the hatching pheasant-covers,
When, that now the grass is tedded,
Loving lad and lass are wedded,
And we stack and thatch the clover,
Then the sweet springtime is over,

URANIA.

Over, over,

FRANKLIN.

Over, over ;

ALL.

Then the sweet springtime is over.

URANIA *sings.*

When the brooks are brimmed and bawling,
When the leaves are falling, falling,
When the threshing-flail is lifted,
When the wheat is bruised and sifted,
When the reaper swathes his sickle,
When the cider-presses trickle,
When we rake and burn the rubble,
When the stripling hunts the stubble,
Watching Roy, and whistling Rover,
Then the summer days are over,

APRIL.

Over, over,

FRANKLIN.

Over, over ;

ALL.

Then the summer days are over.

FRANKLIN *sings.*

When the slow team scoops the furrow,
Dormice sleep and hedgehogs burrow,
When the roasting chestnuts sputter,
When the house-slut bars the shutter,
When the rain-vat fills and freezes,
When the swineherd coughs and wheezes,
And when homeward to the haggard
Wind the cattle, lowing, laggard,
Followed by the drowsy drover,
Then the autumn days are over,

URANIA.

Over, over,

APRIL.

Over, over ;

ALL.

Then the autumn days are over.

FORTUNATUS *sings.*

When the lambing ewes are hurdled,
When the cream floats rich and curdled,

I

When the throstle trills and trebles,
When betwixt the shining pebbles
And the runnel past them sailing
Poiseth, motionless, the grayling;
When the primrose-sheeted covers
Couches are for dreaming lovers,
When the foal and broodmare hinny,
And in every cut-down spinney
Ladysmocks grow mauve and mauver,
Then the winter days are over,

APRIL.

Over, over,

URANIA.

Over, over;

ALL.

Then the winter days are over.

[FRANKLIN, URANIA, and FORTUNATUS spend the afternoon
in the hayfield, helping to rake up the hay, and to pile
it on the wains. When the last cart is loaded, APRIL,
flushed with exercise and excitement, runs up to
FORTUNATUS.]

APRIL.

Now on this last load must we climb and ride,
Or 'twill be sure to heat.

    [*To* FORTUNATUS.]

       You must mount first,

And drag me and Urania after you.

O yes, Urania! you must ride, you must,

While grand-dad leads the way.

[FORTUNATUS climbs to the top of the wain, and helps APRIL
  and URANIA to do the same. The three then sit on
  the hay, APRIL on FORTUNATUS'S knee, and with her
  arm round his neck. FRANKLIN walks at the horse's
  head. The other haymakers cluster round the cart,
  and, as it moves on to the stack, they all sing.]

  Here's to him that grows it,

    Drink, lads, drink!

  That lays it in and mows it,

    Clink, jugs, clink!

  To him that mows and makes it,

  That scatters it and shakes it,

  That turns, and teds, and rakes it,

    Clink, jugs, clink!

  Now here's to him that stacks it,

    Drink, lads, drink!

That thatches and that tacks it,

         Clink, jugs, clink!

That cuts it out for eating,

When March-dropped lambs are bleating,

And the slate-blue clouds are sleeting,

         Drink, lads, drink!

And here's to thane and yeoman,

         Drink, lads, drink!

To horseman and to bowman,

         Clink, jugs, clink!

To lofty and to low man,

Who bears a grudge to no man,

But flinches from no foeman,

         Drink, lads, drink!

SCENE V

[URANIA's garden. FORTUNATUS is pacing the garden alone.
URANIA comes out of the house, singing.]

URANIA.

Everywhere are roses, roses!

[Seeing FORTUNATUS, she breaks off her song.]

FORTUNATUS.

Indeed there are, and roses without thorns,

Flouting the proverb.   You have meshed delight,
And hold it captive.

URANIA.

It is free to go,
But, having freedom of its wings, it stays,
Or, flitting, swift returns.

FORTUNATUS.

Even like me,
Who, loving liberty, am loth to leave
While you and all your roses are abloom.
Tell me their names.

URANIA.

Their names?   They have no name,
Save of my christening; for I lack the craft
Of learnèd catalogues, so that I know them
Less by their fame than by their character.
This is "Unspoken Love."   Eye it, and say
If it be sponsored fittingly.   To me
Its many-folded petals seem to muffle
Some secret rapture beating at its heart.
Love told is loving tarnished, and this rose
Is of its nature unsurrendering.

There's not the faintest blush upon its cheek,
And only by its incense could you guess
Its dreams are chastely passionate.   It is
A rose enraptured with a thought unshaped,
A longing unconfessed.

FORTUNATUS (*holding out his hand*).

. Give me the rose,
That I may learn from it to hide my love,
Or kiss from it its secret.

URANIA (*touching another rose*).

This is called
"Felicity of Home": a round red rose,
Open as day, domestic as the night,
With never a fancy or a fault to hide;
An unromantic rose, but O so wholesome—
Smell it, and say !—so serviceable-sweet,
That when its frail virginity is shed,
Embalmed with orris, clove, angelica,
Woodruff, and marjoram, it hourly scents
And sanctifies a household, keeps it fresh,
And shows it orderly.

FORTUNATUS.

                  A rose too good
To gather for my wearing.

URANIA.

                  Then there is this,
Fantastically clept "The Poet's Dream":
Yet not without some pardon, for it roams,
Rambles, and climbs, no pillar, porch, nor wall,
Will satisfy its vagrancy; and should
You dare to prune its wanderings, or check
Its heavenward necessity, it dies.
And so I let it gipsy as it will,
Most careless and capricious of the roses,
And therefore most desired; a rose too free
To bloom in bondage.

FORTUNATUS.

                  O wise, wilding, rose ! . . .
You are a fairy godmother, and well
You moralise your garden.

URANIA.

                  'Tis alive ;
And is not our morality akin

With character of bird, and beast, and flower,
Our simpler forebears, in whose face we see
Foreshadowings of man's fuller, graver life?

FORTUNATUS.

You have the Secret.   We are kindred all,
From mindless flower to flowering mind, and this,
Synopsis of the Past.

URANIA.

                    And of the Future
Blossom and bud, perpetually opening.
With Man 'tis always Springtime.

FORTUNATUS.

                              But, with men,
Autumn or Winter, mostly.   Nay, forgive me.
Here in your garden—anywhere with you—
It would be always Summer.

URANIA.

                         Rest you here,
Under the tangle of "The Poet's Dream."
Father will join you shortly.   I must go,
And see if April sleeps.

FORTUNATUS.

Abed already !

I had hoped afresh to fold her on my knee
And feel again the velvet of her cheek.
Can I not see her sleeping?

URANIA.

Not to-day.

There is a feverish current in her veins,
Begotten of the haying and your presence.
She has for you a strange expectancy,
A strange remembering ; and your coming back,
After a timely absence that had seemed
To her imagination endless long,
Hath made mid summer simmer in her blood,
That will in sleep subside.

FORTUNATUS.

Kiss her for me,

Just where the slumbering forehead meets the hair.
And, sleeps she sound come back ! come back !—
    yourself,
Sweeter than all your roses !

[URANIA goes into the house.]

SCENE VI

[FRANKLIN and FORTUNATUS at supper in the garden.]

FRANKLIN.

Our handmaid lingers ; we must sup without her.
Her little one is ailing, and she sits
By April's coverlet. She spread the cloth ;
'Tis we must eat the meal.

FORTUNATUS.

     'Tis often thus,
In this imperfectly adjusted world.

FRANKLIN.

It is for us to adjust it. Man is free
To make it odd or even.

FORTUNATUS.

    Is he free ?
An old-world new-world question, never solved.

FRANKLIN.

Yet surely it is soluble. Man's Will
Is finite like his other faculties,

And, like his other faculties, may be
Dwarfed or expanded.   We are bound, in part,
And, where we are bound, submission unto Fate
Is wise surrender.   But, in part, we are free,
And, in that space of liberty, the Will
May be enlarged by watchful exercise.
No attribute is perfect : why then Will ?
Its imperfection is its life, its strength,
Keeping it active.

FORTUNATUS.

          Action ! action ! action !
The orator's receipt is likewise yours ;
And I by action have expelled to-day
Invaders of the mind's serenity.
But would all forms of action thus suffice ?

FRANKLIN.

No, action may be noble or ignoble,
And only noble action breeds content,
Refreshment, and repose.   The noblest is
The peasant's and the poet's : loftiest, this ;
That, the most even and accessible.

FORTUNATUS.

Have poets then refreshment and repose?
Are they content?

FRANKLIN.

　　　　　¡Wise poets needs must be;
Feeling most keenly, understanding best,
With ampler vision, deeper scrutiny,
And fantasy more soaring; firmer grasp
Of this substantial earth, more frequent glimpse
Of that Beyond, the lightnings of the mind
Open by fitful flashes; crowning all,
The articulate delight of Orphic song,
That seems to solve the riddles of the world
With musical responses.

FORTUNATUS.

　　　　　But, alas!
Poets are few, and poets that are wise
Are—well, where *are* they?   Sleeping in their graves.

FRANKLIN.

Or, haply, in their cradles; and, meanwhile,
To be a peasant, wise or otherwise,

Is no ill lot. The uncertain certainty
Of the recurring seasons gives to Will,
Action, and hope, unfailing appetite,
With ample fare to feed on. The last sheep
Was scarcely shorn, when scythes had to be ground;
And almost ere the wheaten sheaves be stacked,
The hops, as though aware that food and drink
Are twin, if drink the younger, fill the air
With hints of homely banquets yet to be.

FORTUNATUS.

But leisure, change, and travel,—are not these
Auxiliaries of wisdom, full as needed
As work, and will, and Nature's discipline?

FRANKLIN.

Yes, lest we wax too trite and circular.
Thrice hath Urania pastured in the vales,
The cherry-peopled vales, moist, green, and cool,
Scooped by the rivalry of Alp with Alp,
And, times uncounted, have we reaped together
The endless harvest of the golden towns
That ripen in the sun of Italy;

And oftener still we have ploughed our native land
With the keen edge of curiosity,
Whetted by born affection.   But the wise
Live anchored mostly, and in wanderings rare
Find confirmation of the bliss of home ;
And rustic service leaves them ample space
For helpful holiday.

FORTUNATUS.

But in these lone
Sequestered silences of chase and pool,
This wildwood realm of antiquated boughs,
But tenanted by foxglove and by fern,
Wherein you hedge your honeysuckled home,
Though Love might brood there aptly, only doves
Ponder on constancy, or dappled does,
Fair damsels of the forest-glade, disport
Their beauty inaccessible and gleam
Coy phantoms of possession.

FRANKLIN.

Who shall say ?
In intervals of fancy have I deemed
That, in a world pure-fashioned by the Will,

Love would be each one's secret, known of none
Save the belovëd ; and the wise who are strong,
Even in this conditioned sphere of sense,
Nest like the nightingale, which, rarely seen,
In curtained joy instinctively abides.
Love is a rustic, almost a recluse,
A haunter of the gloaming and the dew,
Lit by the evening star.   In arid towns,
Lust borrows the vocabulary of Love,
And masquerades romantically till
Day doffs the domino.   Better abide,
Unloving and unloved, in lonely lanes
Yet knowing well what Love is, than consor
With meretricious mummers.

FORTUNATUS.

                           See, the moon,
Unneeded by the summer night, whose way
Is lighted half by lingering yesterday,
Half by approaching morrow, glistens through
The intercepting leaves.   I must away,
And carry through the lengthening forest-tracks
Remembrance and regret.

SCENE VII

[FORTUNATUS is leading his horse to the garden gate. Just ere
he reaches it, URANIA stands before him in the moonlight.
He tethers his horse, and leans with her over the gate.]

URANIA.

The moon will bear you company to-night,
And silver with her half-superfluous beams
Your sylvan journey.

FORTUNATUS.

                    Would that it were you,
Suspended not in Heaven, too like to her,
But earthly as myself, who shared my ride
Through fantasies of forest.
                    [He gazes at her.]
                    White, pure white,
All save the glimmering hair, and that one rose
Promoted to your breast! Sleeps she, then, sound,
That you have quit your vigil to console
The solitary night?

URANIA.

                    She slumbers, husht,
The kiss between her forehead and her hair,

Remembered as your message, having stilled
The ripple of her questions.

FORTUNATUS.

Wherefore, then,
Roamed you in veiled felicity aloof,
Denying us your voice?   Our converse lacked
The minor key, too masculine throughout,
And therefore inconclusive.

URANIA.

There are thoughts,
Need silence to be listened to, and such
Were mine to-night, unfitted to compete
With definite debate.

[Suddenly a nightingale sings overhead.]

How late in June
Flutes that contiguous nightingale, so soon
To flute no more!

FORTUNATUS.

Alas! romantic bird!
Now buxom Summer swelters 'mong her swathes,
The homely misselthrush will sing you down,
And every ditty will be heard save yours.

K

URANIA.

Why dwell you on these contrasts, sad in thought,
And scarce, in language, manifest ?   To me,
The nightingale is jocund as the lark,
The lark pathetic as the nightingale,
Both, sweet as sadness, sad as sweetness' self.

FORTUNATUS.

I wish that you could make my sadness sweet,
As well indeed you might.   Within your voice
Despondency subsists not, and your thoughts,
Mildly imperious as the morning sun,
Banish from life its misty mournfulness.

URANIA.

It is your fancy crowns me.   Use it, rather,
To lift yourself unto the sovran throne
Of cheerful wisdom.

FORTUNATUS.

                         So I might, if you
Would deign to be its consort, or permit
Me, lowlier, to be yours.   Urania !
I never thought to love again, or lose

The sense of loneliness high longings breed,
Unshared, unsatisfied, so half forsworn.
Absolve me for that faithlessness, now I,
Beholding you, return unto my faith,
And, humble penitent, confess that Love,
Begotten by the mind upon the heart,
Not the mere waif of fantasy or sense,
Can liberate life's longings, and redeem
Material servitude.　And yet—and yet—
What if the fancy, and the senses too,
Enforce their claim, and fervid youth revived
By spell of hazel hair, of hazel eyes,
Need the old words—"I love you!—Sweet! be mine!"—
No wonder that I stammer, for my heart
Is where my voice should be—the old, old words,
The old, old want, yet different from the old,
As you from all else differ—highest, best—
And, highest, best, most longed-for and most loved!

[He lays his hand on hers.]

URANIA.

Why did we listen to that nightingale
Or I to you?　We cannot answer it,
Though it be preternaturally sweet ;

And I with selfish ears, spell-bound and husht,
Have hearkened to your heart, forgetting quite   .
Mine may not set its music unto yours.

        [He withdraws his hand.]

Nay, do not take your tenderness away.
Listening, I sometimes think that you are he
Who found my nature long ago, and holds
It captive in his own.

FORTUNATUS.

Are you betrothed ?

URANIA.

I am betrothed to him, not he to me.

FORTUNATUS.

Knows he your troth ?

URANIA.

No, nor will ever know it,
Save some celestial accident reveal
Our oneness to each other.

FORTUNATUS.

And shall this,
This mirage of the mind, this viewless vision,

This covenant uncovenanted, seal
The avenues of choice to living love,
Here faltering on your threshold, suing low
For leave to cross it ?

URANIA.

                    Sue not, I beseech you !
There is persuasion in your voice, and I
Must never be persuaded.   O sir, see !
It is not suitable that you should plead
To one who still would nothing have to give
Had she the giving of it.   It is not mine,
Or—well, it should be yours.   You are sad, but noble,
Your nobleness your own, while my poor wisdom
Is echoed from my sire.   I am not wise ;
I am nothing, save, for a moment, the bright cheat
Imagination makes me.

FORTUNATUS.

                    See you him often ?

URANIA.

I see him always ; were it not for him,
I should see nothing else.   He hath become
A portion of my sight as of my thought.

Hark ! how again yon nightingale propels
Its yearning upward !   'Tis his voice I hear.
He wanders in the garden, he abides
In every rose ; and when the autumn leaves
Huddle in shallows of my winding walks,
I think myself his comfort, if he came,
As come he doth not, to keep winter warm.
Ofttimes I fancy April is his child,
No more a woodland waif unparented,
That I may love and tend her for his sake.

FORTUNATUS.

I would that I were he !

URANIA.

                    I would you were !
But if I falsely welcomed you for him,
He would be gone, and you have banished him.
How could I love you, then ? . . . Go—go—before—
Nay, stay a little while, that I may know
You quit me not with feet of bitterness.
I should have loved you, had I loved not him.
I was so happy : I am hapless now.

    [She withdraws her hand, and half repels him.]

There!   Go!   There is no magic in the moon
To lighten such a darkness!

FORTUNATUS (*folding his arms round her, and looking
intently into her face*).

Nay! attend!
Be this not love, it mimics it so close,
I will not take your answer.

URANIA.

But you must!
I do *not* love you.

FORTUNATUS (*liberating her*).

Wherefore should you love,
In deed or dream, you born but to be loved?
It is a wasteful world, wherein we see
The loveliest apparitions suddenly dropped
By Time, the gaoler of Eternity,
Into the dark deep oubliette of death;
And Time will be oblivious of this hour.
But when the elder whitens at your gate,
As now it doth, in undiscovered years,
And some belated nightingale laments

The pity of this night . . .

Remember that I loved you.

[He kisses her forehead, mounts his horse, then looks back
a moment.]

Latest and loveliest of my dreams, farewell !

SCENE VIII

[FORTUNATUS reins in his horse from a gallop, and advances
through the forest at a foot's pace.]

FORTUNATUS.

"There is no magic in the moon," she said,

"To lighten such a darkness."   What is dark,

What, light ? what, life ? what, death ? save shifting
　　　shadows,

Now come, now gone, with movement meaningless !

"I was so happy : I am hapless now."

That change will change afresh, to change again,

In sterile oscillation.   Thus we pass,

With mere monotonous mutability,

From cradle unto sepulchre, the van

Of other shadows, fleeting as ourselves.

Yet the boughs seem more luminous to-night,

Because she lives !   Paceth she still the garden,

Regretfully remindful? or recurs

To him, the unforgotten?   Doth she gaze

On April's sleep, and her unravelled hair

Fall in unmurmuring ripples to her feet?

Nay, but surmise no more: the truth's enough!

Imagination makes it but more bitter.

[He again breaks into a gallop, till he reaches a round clear-
ing in the forest, where he sees ABADDON sitting on the
ground, surrounded by a circle of twenty-four glowworms.
ABADDON raises his hand deprecatingly, that the silence
may not be broken.   Shortly he rises to his feet, with an
exclamation of impatience.]

ABADDON.

I never knew that spell to fail before.

FORTUNATUS.

What spell, nocturnal wizard?

ABADDON.

                  Sooth, the spell

Of male desire and female vanity,

The most infallible philtre ever brewed.

But you have thrown your vantages away,

And handicap my cunning.   Why, an oaf

That never handled anything more dainty

Than the plough's tail, had done the business better.

FORTUNATUS.

What business, pray?

ABADDON.

Your business, Duke, and mine:
Appropriation of as rare a piece
Of comeliness and virtue as the world
Has seen since Eve found Eden wearisome.
The Serpent managed better, though he had
No odds like yours.   A maiden all recluse,
And yet to you accessible ;—to you !—
A sultry summer night, scented and still,
Enchanted by the dewy moon, the wail
Of a fond faltering nightingale ;—what more
Could the most amorous pessimist conceive,
To second his seductions?

FORTUNATUS (*springing from his horse, and seizing*
ABADDON *by the throat*).

Fool or fiend !
Caitiff or conjuror !   Do you dare avow
You eavesdropped to our colloquy, and lurked,
A listener at the gate !
                [Withdrawing his grip.]
                Your windpipe's iron !

ABADDON.

You cannot choke the Devil. . . . Beside, good
    Duke,
Mingle a little reason with your wrath.
How could I now conceivably be here,
Circled by these my shining servitors,
If I had ambushed by Urania's garden
To intercept your secret? You have fled
From the lost battle hotly, for I heard
Your horse-hoofs hammering hollow on the sod
As I sate here divining. Come! be fair.
We have been partners often, though you gave
But little thought to your auxiliary,
And many a melting morsel have you owed
To the concurrence of the *Pride of Life*,
When *Lust of the Flesh* unaided must have fed
On its own appetite. But now when I
Crave, just for once, your potency in turn,
You abdicate your eminence, and sue
In sentimental syllables as though
You were a mendicant and she a queen.
Why, a shock-headed yokel of the wain,
Concupiscent chawbacon, would have lagged

Longer than you, seducing maiden pique
And curiosity to whet themselves
Upon the edge of waiting.   Words—words—words !
And with no action suited to the word !
Oft thus are women wooed, but never won.

FORTUNATUS.

True love is simple.

ABADDON.

           Ay, a simpleton,
And hence receives a simpleton's reward.
I do believe you would have married her !

FORTUNATUS.

What reverence offers, that I offered her,
Leaving her nature sovran arbiter
Anent the ceremonial shows of love.

ABADDON.

And happily she foils, by her refusal,
Your courtly homage.   We are baffled, both !
I by your simpleness, and you by hers.
Enough to vex a saint, do men not say ?
Then think how it must irritate the Devil !

FORTUNATUS.

Whom are you bent to injure ? her, or me ?

ABADDON.

To injure !   Nay, you rate yourself too cheap.

You would have lured her most bewitchingly,

Had you but longed for her less, and she been lulled

By the enchantment of the luscious lie,

Till—well, till fancy flags.   But you, an expert

In evanescent rapture, needs must crave

Monotony of wedlock, and exchange

A week of kisses for a life of yawns,

O Duke, turned dotard !

FORTUNATUS.

                    You are the Devil indeed !

ABADDON.

Reproach me not.   I am the *Pride of Life*,

And follow my vocation.   Where is the man,

Doglike submissive when you flout his trade,

As mine is flouted by Urania ?

Poor devil ! poor duke ! for you are flouted too,

And I disdained in lordly company.

FORTUNATUS.

What do you with those lanthorns of the ground,
Now when the moon monopolises heaven,
And every leaf whereon is globed the dew
Shines like a little cup of liquid light ?

ABADDON.

Because her too effulgent beams have paled
Heaven's dwarfer orbs, and these terrestrial stars,
Collated by my necromancy, yield
A kindred revelation.   Not alone
By constellation or the wayward flight
Of wild goose and of mallard, or the croak
Of marish frog, or palimpsest of palm,
But by all correlated shows of life,
Movement, or law, can patient subtlety
Construct an alphabet whereby mind may
Surmise in part the vague significance
Of enigmatic Nature. ... . Test their power,
Propounding them some question.   If they answer,
Their mellow phosphorescence comes and goes
In legible pulsations : they are ranged
In order alphabetical that rounds
To Omega from Alpha.

FORTUNATUS.

Who is he,

Urania loves?

ABADDON.

That, will they not disclose,

Save that you have some spell to me unknown

To intimidate their secret.   I have plied

With incantations of the earth and air

Their steadfast cressets, and they will not wink

The faintest intimation.   Hold have I none

Over the uncarnal motions of the mind,

Which, till allied with matter, do not find

A lurking-place in casual substances

That may betray them.

FORTUNATUS.

Ply them again, withal,

And bid them answer whom Urania loves.

ABADDON.

Now the slowworm slimes the path,
Now the bat leaves belfry lath
And about the midgy air
Flitters for its midnight fare ;

Now within the greasy hut
Woodman snores beside his slut,
Now the noiseless barn-owl flaps
Along rick and hedgerow-gaps,
Swerving where the shrewmouse naps ;
Now the mouldwarp quits its burrow,
Groping up the covered furrow
Till the knotted worms are seen
Glittering in the moonlight sheen ;
Now the night-jar sits and saws,
And the vixen licks her paws,
Home-come from the rifled roost ;
Now the mill-stream flows unsluiced ;
Now the hedgehog slinks for food
For its deaf and purblind brood,
Gnaws the viper by the tail,
Sucks the egg or sniffs the pail ;
Now the weevils cluster thick
'Neath the puckered agaric ;
Every glowworm, light her link,
And, as I command you, wink
Who it is Urania loves !

See ! see ! their little cruses fill with fire,

And flicker revelation.   Read them ! quick !
They answer—FORTUNATUS.

FORTUNATUS.

But She hath answered that she doth not love me.

ABADDON.

'Tis likelier that a woman lies than they,
Or that they ken what she herself ignores.
Ply them again—now—now that they are trim
To signify their secrets. . . . Sceptic duke !
Let me interrogate their burnished wicks,
And force from them the undiscovered thoughts
That haunt the Underworld.   Respond anew,
Who begat April, Springtime's castaway ?
Look ! look again ! how every lettered light,
Like to a coruscating topaz, flows,
Then ebbs with mystic meaning.   Eye them sharp,
They answer—FORTUNATUS.

FORTUNATUS.

                 Press them then
Who was the mother that unmothered her,
Abandoned 'mong the bluebells ?

ABADDON.

                              Look ! they swoon,
And darken in their sockets, as though you had,
By pressing them too close, extinguished them.
There ! they are out !

FORTUNATUS.

                              But conjure them again,
And make them throb oracularly till
That parentage be known.   I'll ask no more.

ABADDON.

You might as well interrogate the stars
In day's meridian, as enforce their light
When once they are sunk and set.
   [He gathers up the glowworms, and scatters them broadcast.]
                              Nay, let them keep
Their secret news in bank and holly-bush,
Till next I summon them.   But come, your Grace,
We two might puzzle out, without their aid,
This mystery of motherhood, so you
Will call your past affections to the task.
Remember you The Nameless One ?

FORTUNATUS.

                              Alack !
Plainlier than any ever named or known.

ABADDON.

Ay, ay, because she left you ;—you more wont
To leave than be relinquished.   Men remember
When they're forgotten ; when remembered, they
Themselves forget.   But wherefore did she quit you ?

FORTUNATUS.

Because she sought to reign upon my hearth,
And share the sceptre of the marriage-ring,
And I denied her ; for in truth she was
No blossom of my plucking, but a flower
Another had culled and thankless thrown away
As children drop their posy once 'tis gathered.
Yet half the freshness of the bud still lurked
In her unhulled virginity, and since
I tenderly disposed her, she conceived
There was no abdication I would not
Sign for another smile, poor Nameless One !

ABADDON.

True was her tale then! though they ofttimes lie,
Dissembling their own waywardness.　　　　.

FORTUNATUS.

　　　　　　　　But how
Heard *you* her tale?

ABADDON.

　　　　　She faded in my care.
The wriggling worms have got her beauty now,
Paying no tax for their propinquity,
Yet more familiar with her costly flesh
Than any the richest, rarest, of you all.
She loved you best, because you were a duke;
And yet she loved you best.　That way they love,
Just as they love to lie beneath a quilt
Of ostentatious softness.　Had a Prince
But come her way, she would have loved him better.
But, since none did so—well, you were her Prince,
Until she could not wheedle you withal
To label her a Princess.　Then she fled,
But not alone, projecting to return

And cozen you more femininely when
The hope within her womb smiled on her breast.

FORTUNATUS.

What of the child?

ABADDON.

It smiled, but never there!
Finding an orphan darkness in the light
Its mother gave it, as herself went out.

FORTUNATUS.

But what to you was mother, or babe, or——

ABADDON.

Nay!

The Devil is not ungrateful, and I thus
Paid her for many an innocent her lips
Had kissed into perdition.   By my pack!
I know not, of the twain, if she or you
Have served more fruitfully the *Pride of Life*
And *Lust of the Flesh*; and so I took the babe,
And, when matured to winsomeness, exposed

Its dimples in the primroses where next

Urania, foresting, was timed to pass.

[A troop of unbroken colts come galloping through the
forest, and startle FORTUNATUS's horse. He goes to
quieten and secure it.   Returning, he finds ABADDON
has vanished.]

FORTUNATUS.

What ho !

A VOICE.

What ho !

FORTUNATUS (*mounting his horse*).

I'll gallop through the forest, till I find

This juggling newsman of the night.

[As he breaks into a gallop, he sees, emerging from an
avenue, a hundred yards ahead, but at right angles to
that along which he is himself advancing, ABADDON, astride
of one of the wild colts, tearing along at full speed, followed by the whole troop.]

FORTUNATUS.

What ho !

ABADDON.

What ho ! lord duke !   Come on ! and race the
     Devil !

SCENE IX

[URANIA'S garden. URANIA is pacing slowly, in the moonlight ;
shortly she is joined by her father.]

FRANKLIN.

Is April sleeping ?

URANIA.

Yes, refreshingly.

FRANKLIN.

Observe you not a likeness in the curves
About her mouth and his, though plastic hers,
And his arrested by the serious years?

URANIA.

Mere fancy, father !   Rather should I say,
Were that not yet more fanciful, that he
In voice and lineament re-echoes you.

FRANKLIN.

Your fancy for my fancy ; futile both :
Though verily I marvelled when to-day
He trolled our song, and chimed the final strophe

Familiarly as we?   I never knew
A voice that was not of my kindred chant
That local ditty carolled by my nurse,
And by me taught to April and to you.
Who may he be?

URANIA.

He is Duke Fortunatus

FRANKLIN.

That is he not! . . . Urania, let us sit,
While I to you disclose what haply you
Will deem I might have whispered you before.
Hear first the tale, and, when the tale is told,
The plea shall follow. . . . I am Duke Fortunatus;
And thus it seems he must be of my kin.
Sick in my youth of splendour, but too weak
To bear its burdens sternly, I resolved
To shuffle that luxurious fardel off
To other shoulders, and myself assume,
Unknown to all, the lowlier tasks that mate
With Understanding and wise Happiness.
Perhaps it was a selfish abdication;
Withal, a selfishness I cannot rue.
I vanished, and the world conceived me dead.

The dukedom to a distant kinsman passed,
Who gloried in his trappings, but enjoyed
His harness briefly; unto whom, 'twould seem,
Succeeded he we entertained to-day.
I to myself sufficiency reserved
For study and for travel;—last, for home,
Here where your mother died and you were born.
Why did I hug my secret?   Sweet, forgive!
But if upon the fantasies of pomp
Men gaze with clownish awe, men born with thews
And masculine conceptions, is it strange
That women, daintier in their nerves and needs,
Should reverence vulgar opulence, and rank
That gives to splendour grace and dignity?
Nay, have it as you will; perhaps I wronged you.
Perhaps I wronged your mother.   But I gave,
Not the poor gauds you might have both regretted
And blamed me for withholding, but such wealth
As—nay, 'tis poor—but, rich enough for me,
And so I hoped, child, rich enough for you.

URANIA.

'Tis wealth I would not barter for all titles
And pomp in the world.

FRANKLIN.

              Yet now indeed you must ;
For I discern how deeply I have wronged him.
See ! I have laid upon his life a load
'Neath which he staggers ; so must I resume it,
Now I can carry it as though 'twere not,
And set him free, before it be too late,
To learn to walk erect.

URANIA.

              How sad he seems !
So sad, that I myself could almost weep
His unsubstantial sorrow.

FRANKLIN.

              Find him woe.
His sense of happiness will wake when grief
Hath half withdrawn her curtain.   Well, good-night,
And more of this to-morrow.

SCENE X

[Midnight.   URANIA's chamber.]

APRIL (*sleepily*).

Urania, has he gone ?   Ask him to come :
I want to say good-night before he goes.

URANIA.

He is deep within the forest, long ere this.
Hark ! that is midnight strikes.

APRIL.

        I am so sorry.
When will he come again ?

URANIA.

        Nay, you must sleep.
Lie still, and close your eyes.
        [APRIL drops off again into slumber.]
        Ay, when ?   When ?   When !
" Latest and loveliest of my dreams, farewell ! "
'Twas thus he left me.   We are dreamers, both.
Yet never farewell to mine ! which neither time.
Nor the seductions of a visible presence
Can banish from my gaze.   Had he but sued
Before the dedication of my thought
To one exclusive longing, it is sure
His heart's vibration would have sounded mine,
And made harmonious what's discordant now.
With what a lonely dignity he breathed
His hope, with what sad dignity resigned !

O, I am crimsoned with confusion, when

I hear again his halting utterance

Accompany the nightingale, and think

'Tis he that asked, and I that dared withhold !

And yet the consecrated past forbids

A less unnatural answer.

> [She takes the volume out of which she previously read, and folds it to her heart as she composes herself to sleep.]

O my love !

Lie in the bosom of my sleep to-night,

So I may still be lapped in constancy,

And know no other dream but thee,—but thee !

END OF ACT II

ACT III

SCENE I

[URANIA's garden.]

URANIA (*alone at the gate*).

Would he were here ! though haply, when he comes,
His presence will be only pitying pain.
No, now he is my kinsman.   That saves all,
And he with that sweet bond will be content,
And love be loved in consanguinity.
Once that delirious dreams from April's sleep
Are patiently dissolved, how she will joy
To find he is no stranger.   Hark ! . . . But no !
We hear that which we listen for, and hope
Befools like fear.

[She leans over the gate, reading.   As she does so,
FORTUNATUS gallops up.]

FORTUNATUS.

How—how—is April? Take me to her straight.

URANIA.

Forbear, a little while! for, when she wakes,
The fever flames afresh, and thought of you,
So curiously dominant, recurs
Through her meanderings of speech and song.
I left her, sleeping, but a moment since,
To hearken for your hoofs.   I little deemed,
When yesternight I heard them faint and fade
Into the forest avenues, I should   .
So soon again be straining toward their tread.

FORTUNATUS.

I should have come unsummoned, though your
        message
Quickened my advent.   For my midnight ride
Through the illuminated woodland brought
Pathetic revelation which your ears
Must hearken, and your tenderness forgive.
I—I—am April's father!

URANIA (*starting back*).

> And her mother?

FORTUNATUS.

Is where that father oft would fain have been,
And, but for April, now too fain would be,
Absolved in death.

URANIA.

> You loved her?

FORTUNATUS.

> That, I did not;
Or loved her—well, as men too often love,
When haplessly they may not love at all,
Yet cannot live without love's counterfeit.

URANIA.

But how could you forsake her, when her life——

FORTUNATUS.

Forsake her?   Nay, you wrong me.   It was she
Who left me, claiming marriage, having no claim
Through guile, or guilt, or promises of mine;

Deeming—last night I newly heard—to prove
The force of my refusal when she might
Sue at my heart with April in her arms.
She died,—a mother; and Abaddon laid—
So he avouches—April in the wood,
With purpose—fair or fiendish, who shall say?—
That you should foster her.   How came he thus
To tamper with my fate, I did not learn;
For, just as I was probing him for more,
The moonlight madcap vanished in the chase,
Astride of one of its unbitted colts,
And, though on him I pressed with leaning speed,
In winding of the ways I lost his trail,
And tell a gaping story,—withal true.

URANIA.

Never did pity tell a sadder tale.
Peace to the dead! forgiveness to the living!
Forgiveness, and compassion.

FORTUNATUS.

                              Sister mine!
Nay, foster-wife, for April's foster-mother,

I have no feud with present or past that knits
Our lives so fondly.   What is it you read?

[He takes the book from her.]

Where did you get this volume?

URANIA.

From Abaddon.

I bought it from his pack, three summers since,
Just as my nature budded to receive
Its sunshine and its dew, its wandering winds
Of music and of magic, light and shade
Of solemn joy and hopeful sorrowing,
The poet's message, comforting the sad,
Admonishing the happy.   From that hour,
Its thoughts enrich my poverty, its verse
Grafts on my growth a glory not my own.

FORTUNATUS.

Know you who wrote it?

URANIA.

If I knew but that,
Then—nay, 'tis better that I should not know.

M

But, if I knew, and if he lived—why, then—
But ask me nothing further.   What I know,
I told last night.   Forgive me ! but my heart
Irrevocably is to him betrothed
Who first unsealed my nature through this book.

FORTUNATUS.

'Twas I that wrote it !

URANIA.

Is it true ?

FORTUNATUS.

As true

As time and as remembrance ! ay, as true,
Urania, as your heart, and as my love !

SCENE II

[Three days later.]

FRANKLIN.

Yes, I have pondered deeply, and the last
Conclusion of reflection but confirms

The first arrest of instinct.   It must be.
Reluctant shall I quit this narrow plot,
Long co-extensive with the world, and leave
You and Urania, wedded, to maintain
Its shy felicity.   Duties there are,
Imposed upon the Present by the Past,
And not to be foregone.   I see that, now ;
And them I will discharge, for they are mine,
Till time shall come they will in turn be yours.
Prepare for them by labour, by disdain
Of accidental splendour, by faith, hope,
Love, constancy, and joy in simple joys.
But, above all, foster Humility.
For Pessimism, latest, lewdest birth
Of Pride of Life and Lust of the Flesh——

FORTUNATUS.

How strange !

Abaddon arrogated those twin names
In many a mocking utterance.

FRANKLIN.

Then he was
An honest Devil.

FORTUNATUS.

But do you conceive

Him other than a pedlar?

FRANKLIN.

Who shall say?

Voices there are, and spectres plausible,

Fantastic simulations suddenly flashed

From the retentive Underworld, and they

Who own these not have but imperfect senses.

Demon or pedlar, he proclaimed a truth

By his self-christening.   Therefore, kinsman dear,

Before you lead Urania to her hearth,

Wend with her meekly to the village Church,

And, stooping low, pass through the little door,

Door of Humility, that April named,

And kneel, as others kneel, the poor, the simple,

And celebrate your nuptials even as they.

That which we know, tenaciously must be,

Tenaciously if meekly, not forsworn.   .

But the Unknown deny not, and revere

The circumambient mystery that inspires

With kindly curtain our foreshadowing dreams,

And, when in individual darkness, seek

The light of Universal Piety.

Is it not plain the experienced Past must be

Wiser than any Present, and mankind

Surer than you or I?   My Mother strove,

With love, with admonition, with reproof,

To make me humble, and alas! in vain.

Life has enforced the lesson. . . . But I keep you.

Urania beckons from the casement.   Go.

SCENE III.

[URANIA's chamber.]

URANIA (*to* APRIL).

Sweet! he is here, and wants to talk with you.

APRIL.

Then, now we can take the swarm.   A swarm in
May, a swarm—— But you have not brought the
beanstalk, Urania; so grand-dad will have to take
it.   I don't like that story; it's too sad.   But they
can sip the honeyed wine.   What a dear beautiful
Queen!   Poor leper!

FORTUNATUS.

Thus do the equitable hours avenge
Our wayward purposes, just as we scan
Their true-appointed goal !   She does not know me.

URANIA.

Love ! it is he you sent for, he that laid
Your cheek against his cheek upon the wain,
And told you pretty stories.

APRIL.

This is not broken meat ; these are myrtles.   What
a wicked king !   The bees are in your hair, Urania ;
and yet I limed the hive with hydromel.   When will
he come again ?

FORTUNATUS.

See ! I am here ; and never to depart.
You know me, do you not ?

APRIL.

Yes, a most lovely lady.   Suppose they were to
slay you ?   Is my new frock ready, Urania ?   Because,
you know, he is coming.

URANIA.

Thus did she wail and wander through the night.

[Taking APRIL in her arms.]

Nay, let me try to lullaby her tongue.
Sleep, angel! sleep!

FORTUNATUS.

Alas! there is no ditty,
No note nor incantation of despair,
Can rock her random musings. . . . Now, you know
    me?

APRIL.

Yes, dear grand-dad.   If you love me, stay in
Heaven, and shine above me.   Now we have housed
them snug and warm, have we not?   Urania, read
from that pretty book about the stars.

URANIA.

Your book, she means; the volume that betrothed,
With its premonitory spell, my life
Insensibly to yours.   She loves to hear
Verse that she understands not.

FORTUNATUS.

Is that sure?
Haply she apprehends what you who read,
And I who wrote, farther from Heaven than she,
Miss of its meaning.

APRIL.

But we must sing it, all together, you know. Shall
I begin?   When the ladysmocks have faded.   I
forget the rest.   O, I remember now!
Over, over!
Now the April days are over!

FORTUNATUS.

See! now she sleeps.

URANIA.

Only to wake in Heaven!

END OF ACT III

ACT IV

SCENE I

[Terrace of the DUKE's castle. The DUKE, with ADRIAN
at his side; the household standing round, and the
dwellers on the estate assembled in front.]

DUKE (*to* ADRIAN).

Nay, Adrian, be my secretary, now.
Yet take it not amiss if ofttimes I
Trespass upon your functions; for there are
Duties too personal to be discharged
By the most capable and kindly vicar.
Therefore, I pray you, aid me constantly,
But do not let me abdicate.   Myself,
Since Heaven is pleased to name me for the task,
Must learn, with eyes and ears not yours but mine,
The needs of them who, be it kindly said,
Depend on me, on whom I do depend.

[*To the* VICAR.]

Help me, good Vicar!   I will help you always.

[*To the* SCHOOLMASTER.]

And you who have these little ones in charge,
I pray you, teach them virtue, love of country,
Faith, Hope, and Charity, the Graces Three,
And Reverence, that "angel of the world."
And, so you will permit me, I at times
Will lift the schoolhouse latch and second you
In loving admonitions.

[*To the* CROWD.]

Comrades all!
Who dwell upon the land that's labelled mine,
Though mine it is not more than it is yours,
Give me your friendship, own me for your friend,
And I will do for you, through good and ill,
Whate'er would not undo your manliness,
Derange the commonwealth, nor mar the State.

THE RUSTICS.

Now shall we sing?

DUKE.

I pray you.

ADRIAN.

Now!   Begin!

The PLOUGHMEN *sing.*

Three cheers for Winter,
   That blows upon the horn,
That makes the branches splinter,
   And threshes out the corn :
When chimney-stacks are shaken,
   And flooded is the ditch,
And the gammer salts the bacon,
   And the lasses sit and stitch,
Or thread the melted tallow
   To cheer the longsome nights,
And the ploughland oozeth fallow,
   And the black frost nips and bites ;
When we close and bar the shutter,
   As the wet winds wail and sob,
And we watch the chestnuts sputter
   And crackle on the hob ;
When the Yule log lights the rafter,
   And the gossip tells the tale,

And the house is filled with laughter,
  And the mugs are filled with ale :
      Three cheers for Winter !

       The SHEPHERDS *sing.*

Three cheers for Springtime,
  That makes the pastures strong,
When, blithe upon the wing, Time
  Comes bursting into song :
When celandine and oxslip
  Are dotted all about,
And the young ones on their frocks slip,
  And sally forth and shout ;
When lifted is the wattle,
  And emptied is the shed,
And the dewy-fetlocked cattle
  Roam afield for board and bed ;
When we ply the rake and harrow,
  And bark the oaken bole,
And the lean sow drops her farrow,
  And the broodmare drops her foal ;
When the buxom lambs are bleating,
  And the cuckoo never stops,

And the glad swain and his sweeting
   Are cuddling in the copse :
      Three cheers for Springtime !

     The MOWERS *sing.*

Three cheers for Summer,
   When posies smell once more,
And morrice-man and mummer
   Come dancing to the door :
When open stands the casement,
   And walls that dripped with snow
Are hung from eave to basement
   With roses all ablow ;
When grass is scythed and tedded,
   And work is paid-for play,
And lad and lass are wedded,
   And tumble in the hay ;
When everything increases,
   And mother makes the jams,
While we shear the curly fleeces,
   And wean the lusty lambs ;
When the youngsters pitch the wicket
   Upon the village green,

And the elders watch the cricket
  And talk of what hath been :
    Three cheers for Summer !

   The REAPERS *sing.*

Three cheers for Autumn,
  When jolly shocks of grain,
And the brawny arms that wrought 'em,
  Ride homeward on the wain ;
When the early rime-frost dapples
  The tender woodland leaves,
And the juicy ruddled apples
  Are stored behind the eaves ;
When unto green hop-garden
  Pour all the village folk,
And the cobnuts swell and harden,
  And the oasts are lit and smoke ;
When steams the harvest-supper
  With joints of beef and boar,
And lower dance with upper
  Upon the granary floor ;
When the yeoman counts his earning,
  And the yokel's wage is known,

And the maiden feels a yearning
  For a fireside of her own:
        Three cheers for Autumn!

        They ALL sing.

Then three cheers, my hearties,
  And together three times three,
For whatsoe'er your part is,
  Or whoso ye may be,
Be yours to spud the thistles,
  To scoop and bank the ditch,
To souse and scrape the bristles,
  And to cut up chine and flitch,
To peel and twist the withy,
  To tend the lambing ewe,
To smite upon the stithy
  And hammer out the shoe;
To find the emmet maggots,
  To stake and tie the hops,
Or to stack the hazel faggots
  In spinney and in copse;
To mount the market waggon,
  Or to whistle by the shaft,

Now lift the home-brewed flagon,

And drain a goodly draught :

With three cheers, my hearties !

DUKE.

I never heard a saner song than that,

And its wise wholesomeness may make amends

For something rude and rustic in its rhythm.

These old-world ditties that are handed down

By your ancestral cottages maintain

The tie of time and fellowship alive.

I did not know it.   You must teach it me.

Now shall we in, and cheerly feast together?

SCENE II

[URANIA's garden.]

URANIA.

How quickly, Fortunatus, Love doth learn !

There's not a leaf nor tendril but you know

Its nature by affection ; not a plant

But you dispose it true and tenderly.

FORTUNATUS.

Are they not yours, and were you not my teacher?

URANIA.

They and myself were all I had to give,
And so improve them yours! . . . Have we not
    swept
The borders and the by-paths now enough ;
Dead leaves being part of Autumn's livery,
Befitting more her habit than trim suit
Of modern liking?

FORTUNATUS.

                Yes, the Seasons deck
Themselves in their appropriate garniture ;
Self-conscious Spring betraying its desires
In blushing bud and reddening coppices,
While married Summer, satisfied with home,
Twineth the gadding rose about her brow.
Now widowed Autumn, careless of herself,
And her discoloured garments loosely flying,
Bends all her thought on harvesting the past.
Even Winter, tempering age with dignity,
Over his shoulder flings an ermine cloak,
And calm awaits the End.

                        N

URANIA.

How rightly reasoned,
Now you discern Imagination should
A reconciler, not a rebel, be,
To teach the heart of man to apprehend
Nature's vicissitudes, and bear his own,
With sympathetic fancy.

FORTUNATUS.

Dear Urania!
Next year your garden should be lovelier still,
Now you've an under-gardener.

URANIA.

Next year, alas!
The fairest of our flowers will waken not,
And you must help me to conceive it Spring,
When April doth not bring its namesake back,
To melt the Winter.

FORTUNATUS.

I have kept these blooms
To strew where she abides.

URANIA.

And I saved these.

FORTUNATUS.

Then let us go and sanctify her grave.

URANIA.

But, tell me.   Is the poem not complete?

FORTUNATUS.

It is; and I will read it you to-night.

THE END

Printed by R. & R. CLARK, *Edinburgh*

www.ingramcontent.com/pod-product-compliance
Lightning Source LLC
Chambersburg PA
CBHW030606040726
47497CB00008B/2867